THE MOST BIZARRE CASE IN THE HISTORY OF THE WESTCHESTER SHERIFF'S DEPARTMENT!

He died a bachelor, just eight days short of his 70th birthday, in the midst of the luxurious and sybaritic surroundings he had created for himself during an energetic, full, and sometimes "swinging" bachelor life.

The curious story of Dr. Tarnower's life, his wealth, his success, and his very laid-back lifestyle makes a fascinating one to ponder.

But why would someone want him dead?

Who would kill him?

We will send you a free catalog on request. Any titles not in your local book store can be purchased by mail. Send the price of the book plus 50 cents shipping charge to Leisure Books, P.O. Box 270, Norwalk, Connecticut 06852.

Titles currently in print are available for industrial and sales promotion at reduced rates. Address inquiries to Nordon Publications, Inc., Two Park Avenue, New York, New York 10016, Attention: Premium Sales Department.

THE
SCARSDALE
MURDER

Jay David

LEISURE BOOKS ∞ NEW YORK CITY

A LEISURE BOOK

Published by

Nordon Publications, Inc.
Two Park Avenue
New York, N.Y. 10016

CONTENTS

1

The Murder

Although it resembles in many ways the well-kept, neatly trimmed millionaires' estates in Beverly Hills and Grosse Pointe, Westchester County is unique. Westchester doesn't even compete for the title of the "richest county in the United States" with Fairfield County which adjoins it over the New York/Connecticut state line.

Publicity, competition and a high profile of visibility is not what Westchester wants; it is seclusion and exclusivity. When one drives through the rolling Westchester countryside, one is reminded of the well-manicured landscape of the English countryside in Yorkshire, where gardeners continually work at the vegetation and the residents ride regularly to the hunt, following barking dogs and terrified foxes.

In spite of its generally accepted image, Westchester is schizoid. It includes such bumper-to-bumper towns as White Plains, Yonkers, Mt. Vernon, and New Rochelle, but its image is consistently that of isolated and discreet palatial estates, the kind of terrain described in city zoning ordinances as "larger acreage zoning."

Purchase is typical of areas in Westchester which are made up predominantly of estates for the well-to-do. Purchase itself is actually not a town at all, but a part of the town of Harrison. In fact, Purchase is no more than a post office designation. Harrison was named after John Harrison, the Englishman who bought the land from the King of England in the 1600s, and the map attached to the charter was labeled "Harrison's Purchase." The word "purchase" happened to fall on the northeast section of the Harrison settlement.

The "town" of Purchase has been known by the name ever since—the product of the casual stroke of the plumed quill pen that established the area as the estate of John Harrison.

Nevertheless, most citizens living in the countryside near the Purchase post office consider themselves citizens of Purchase, New York, and have an almost paranoid hunger for privacy. Above all else, they resist real-estate development, and band together uneasily but determinedly in continual battles to keep the zoning laws low in density. This, despite the fact that the pressure of urbanization, particularly the thrust for high-density housing from the great metropolis of New York City to the south, inexorably exerts a negative influence on the estate-dotted countryside.

Three times in the past several years, Purchase has tried to secede from the town of Harrison, of which it is technically a part; but has failed to do so.

Privacy in this area of Westchester County does not denote, as it might seem, any sterility or lack of drama in the lives of those residing there. For the record, it was from one of those large estates that Samuel Bronfman II, the heir to the

Seagram liquor fortune, was kidnapped in 1975 at the home of his mother, Ann Loeb Bronfman. Bronfman was eventually found and released, and his two kidnappers captured, tried, and imprisoned.

And it was out of a large estate only a few miles from there that the limousine carrying Avery Rockefeller Jr. drove just last year, taking to his death the 55-year-old grand-nephew of the late oil magnate John D. Rockefeller in a head-on collision with a car driven by a teenager who had just received his driver's license.

In the Purchase area also live Alfred Knopf, the book publisher, and Ogden R. Reid, former U.S. Representative in Congress and heir to the *Herald-Tribune* fortune.

Only a few hundred yards away from the Bronfman estate lies a 6.2 acre property. On it is situated a large orange brick and glass Japanese-style modern house. In front of the house is a small lake with an island in the center, decorated by a miniature concrete Buddha that faces the house. The Buddha was made in China, where the owner of the house purchased it in 1973.

The house also boasts a swimming pool out in back, and a tennis court near the rear of the property. In addition, there is a vegetable garden that is one of the "sights of the county," according to gourmets who have dined at the house and tasted the delights of the home-grown vegetables and herbs.

The mansion is worth approximately $500,000. It was built in 1958 by Dr. Herman Tarnower, a cardiologist and internist who became an instant celebrity after publishing a diet book. He had developed the special high-protein diet at his offices in the town of Scarsdale nearby, a diet named, appropriately enough, after the clinic he helped found, the Scarsdale Medical Center, and called for that reason the "Scarsdale Diet."

It was in the second-floor bedroom of that home that Tarnower was fatally shot to death on the night of March 10, 1980. He died a bachelor, at the age of 69, just eight days short of his 70th birthday, in the midst of the luxurious and sybaritic surroundings he had created for himself during an energetic, full, and sometimes "swinging" bachelor life.

The detailed truth of what happened in that bedroom just before 11 p.m. on the last night of his life is not actually known. Nevertheless, there are a number of possibilities—and it is generally suspected that his death involved his relationship with the women in his life.

What led to the event that took place that night, and what followed his death add up to one of the strangest and most bizarre cases in the history of the Westchester sheriff's department. Although no conclusions can yet be established because of the court actions which are contemplated at the time of this writing, the curious story of Tarnower's life, his wealth, his success, and his very laid-back lifestyle makes a fascinating one to ponder.

What caused his death?

Why did he die?

Who killed him?

No one really knows—but everyone is allowed to speculate.

* * * *

The winter of 1979-80 had been a disappoint-
ment to hopeful kids with sleds and even ordinary grownups with an eye to the beauty of the
Westchester landscape draped in its usual mantle
of sparkling snow. There was almost no snowfall
that winter. The trees were leafless. The countryside was dull and brown and frozen. The surrounding city governments responsible for plow-
ing the roadways when snow fell were happy not
to have to expend large sums of money out of
already-strained budgets, the average resident
was not happy faced with the mounting cost of
oil, natural gas, and electricity. But in that affluent community no one was signing up for
food stamps yet.

Monday, March 10, 1980, was a gray and
depressing day. By nightfall thunder and lightning and a driving rain were sweeping northward
through Westchester and on up along the eastern
seaboard making life miserable for man and
beast. It was one of those soul-destroying nights
that made transplated Californians shake their
heads and say, "My God, I wish they'd transfer
me back to San Diego, or L.A., or even Marin
County."

The storm lashed at the trees and foliage along
Purchase Street, which meanders through the
plush countryside estates of Westchester County, passing at one point the Tarnower estate. Inside the house Dr. Herman Tarnower was enjoying a quiet dinner with relatives and a close
friend.

Tarnower enjoyed guests. He enjoyed dinner

guests. In fact, he was proud of his own gourmet skills—particularly in dreaming up mouth-watering menus. He had never sweated over an oven in his life, but he knew good food and how it smelled when it was cooking.

With him that night were his sister, Pearl Tarnower Schwartz, his niece, and Mrs. Lynne Tryforos, one of the assistants who worked as his office manager at the Scarsdale Medical Center. It was an intimate group for Tarnower. He was, in fact, quite famed around the area for the numerous guests he invited to his "little but elegant" dinner parties.

It was Monday night. He had his bigger parties either on Friday night or over the weekend. He was hosting this small affair tonight with his usual aplomb in the candle-lit, almost baronial-type dining room in the mansion.

In spite of the intimacy of the group, the setting was very reminiscent of that of an Agatha Christie novel—a sort of 1980 version of the "English country-home" murder mystery of the 1920s, when Christie was turning out her best books and when she was at the peak of her vogue. Here came the affluent and the famous. To their famous host. "Famous," yes: because the whole world now knew Tarnower's name from the fantastic success of his runaway best-seller on dieting. Here tonight were blood relatives and an intimate friend of the host's.

And, melodramatically appropriate, so were the sounds of the menacing storm ripping off tree branches and uprooting brush all around the countryside on the mansion grounds—sound-track equivalent of kettledrum and tympani accompanying the light laughter of

12

the guests and the murmur of conversation.

The scenario was a Christie cliché, too. No one knew that the evening would end in violence, bloodshed, and death. No one knew that Tarnower had only three or four more hours to live. No one knew that everyone at the dinner would be subject to the endless scrutiny of millions of people—in fact, would never be out of the limelight for the rest of their days.

Relaxed, convivial, animated—the dinner boasted the expected sparkling conversation as it always did at Tarnower's house. Although he was all-business in his professional demeanor, Tarnower could be witty, as well as intelligent and perceptive with people he knew and loved.

He lived for these elegant dinners; he led the table talk into all varieties of provocative subjects. He habitually kept things moving by tossing out an engrossing question or statement to stimulate thought and rhetoric.

In the Tarnower household, the art of intelligent conversation was on its way to a triumphal resurrection.

After the party finished their dinner Tarnower led them into the two-level living room to continue their lively talk. Furnished in a comfortable but spare style, the attractive high-ceilinged room was furnished eclectically with traditional artifacts along with many rare objects d'art Tarnower had acquired in his world travels.

And the talk? One can imagine the gamut of subjects:

Was Ted Kennedy actually through in his campaign for the presidency? The press had written him off. So had a number of his advisors. And the White House had scorned his entry into the campaign from the beginning. But the Kennedys had a way of battling against all odds—and coming up winners. After his stunning upset in New York and Connecticut, could he recoup and take the South?

And what about the American hostages in Iran? Had Carter been ill-advised not to move immediately against the terrorists back in November? Would his rose-garden strategy backfire on him eventually? The situation was now becoming more and more desperate for the fifty-odd Americans held in the Embassy. All the civilized world was laughing at Washington. Even the Canadians had outwitted the Iranians and spirited out a handful of Americans; what had happened to the old American nerve and daring?

At one point the talk switched quite suddenly to—you guessed it—murder. The conversation moved on quite quickly afterward, but for those few moments the Agatha Christie fan would recognize immediately the frequently used and classic dramatic device of tragic irony. Tragic irony, for the uninitiated, is a form of dramatic irony in which characters use words or voice ideas that mean one thing to them but have a foreboding meaning to those who understand the situation more completely—especially its aftermath.

The talk about murder involved a novel which dealt with three women who murdered their husbands. As the talk moved back and forth among the principals, Tarnower winked and laughed.

"That's one advantage I have in being a

bachelor," he said, or words to that effect. "It can never happen to me!"

But of course no one there understood the irony of his remark—until the next day.

In spite of the elegance of the conversation, the lilting flow of the talk, the savoring of the excellently cooked food, perhaps one could sense an underlying tension. Was Tarnower's laughter a bit strained? Were his eyes sometimes moving about the room, perhaps unconsciously to a window or a doorway? There seemed to be a presence in the room—the persona of someone not there. Someone who had been there many times before.

Was she out there tonight, sitting in the dark, watching?

Tarnower could not have avoided thinking about Jean Harris because in the past she was said to have sat outside and watched. At least, that was the story that had been making the rounds. Doug Feiden in the *New York Post* reported that she had driven up from her home in Virginia and had remained in the car and watched through the windows as the doctor and his guests had chatted and dined inside. In the cold and the dark she must have sat there isolated and alienated—unable to hear the laughter, unable to join in the bon mots, unable to enjoy the nearness of the man she loved.

Although a bachelor, Tarnower did not live alone. He had a live-in gardener and a live-in cook. The two were married. Henri van der Vreken, a Belgian-born landscape gardener, kept the large estate well-tended. His wife, Suzanne van der Vreken, a French-born painter, acted as Tarnower's cook.

15

As noted, the doctor prided himself on his own ability to select and plan cuisine, but he could not cook at all himself. He supervised Suzanne van der Vreken in many facets of the meal preparation, especially when he had guests, but the actual cooking was left in her capable hands. She was indeed an expert on Continental dishes, particularly in those that separated the gourmet from the gourmand.

Sometime in January or February during a dinner party, the story went, the Belgian gardener had been helping his French wife with the food when he had seen a blue sedan parked outside the house in the long driveway. Van der Vreken knew the car well. The 1973 Chrysler Newport belonged to a long-time friend of Tarnower's. Her name was Mrs. Jean Struven Harris. She was a widow who lived in Virginia and served as headmistress at an exclusive girls' school.

Henri van der Vreken knew that Tarnower had not intended to include Jean Harris in the guest list for the evening. Perhaps she had simply driven up to see Tarnower, not knowing he was entertaining. Van der Vreken went back to his work with his wife, forgetting about the car.

Fifteen minutes later he glanced out the window once again, and noticed the car still there. When he checked in the dining room, he realized that Jean Harris had not come in the house. He studied the car more closely and was a little surprised to see someone sitting inside it. He conferred with his wife. She glanced out, observed the car, and shrugged.

Van der Vreken, the story went, discreetly approached his employer and whispered in his ear that the blue Chrysler, apparently with Jean Harris in it, was outside, and that she seemed to be watching the house. Tarnower froze momentarily, but then recovered and nodded at van der Vreken, telling him that he would investigate. Van der Vreken went back to the kitchen.

According to the report, Tarnower excused himself from his guests and walked down through an inner door that connected the house to the garage. When he pressed the switch to open the garage, the lights of the Chrysler in the driveway flashed on, and the car started up. In a moment it had driven off.

How many times had she been there before, watching him through the window while he was entertaining others he did not know. But the possibility that she might be out there keeping an eye on him must have been totally unnerving. They had been friends for so many years. She was an important part of his life. But so were other people. He was worried about her; he had heard that she was beginning to show signs of anxiety once again at her job.

It was rumored that the two had begun to argue each time they were together. They must have felt that their long-lasting, fourteen-year relationship was beginning to come apart. It might have been the same old story: a woman wanting to marry a man who never planned to marry anyone.

He felt that he was entitled to his freedom. He felt that when he sacrificed the companionship of marriage he deserved to enjoy that freedom. The option to see as many different women as he wanted was part of that freedom. Tarnower had a logical mind. To him it simply did not make

17

sense that Jean Harris could not see it that way; it bothered him that she seemed determined to cause trouble between them.

He still saw her. In fact, he had held a special wedding supper for Jean Harris's youngest son David in February. Why was she bent on disturbing his lifestyle?

Nevertheless, he would naturally feel a bit uneasy about the problems he had heard that Jean Harris was experiencing in her job. She was a strict disciplinarian. And when she was required to exert her authority, some people thought she sometimes overreacted.

He did feel a responsibility for her. Now, with her own personality beginning to change because of their relationship, he was concerned. He was deeply worried about her.

He tried to close his mind to it.

Now, tonight, five days before the Ides of March, it occurred to him that she might be out there once again looking in at him. He knew that the school where she worked was starting its three-week spring vacation. Without her work, she would be at loose ends again. He wondered. . . .

But this time she was not out there. The rest of the evening passed without incident. It was an excellent get-together—it would have been exceptional if it had not be excellent—and by nine o'clock, everyone had gone home. The doctor did not allow himself late hours during the work week. When the time came for the evening to end, there was no excuse for dallying.

His guests departed and Tarnower went upstairs to his bedroom.

At about eleven o'clock that night the van der Vrekens heard what sounded like gun shots and the buzzer from Tarnower's room began to sound in an erratic and almost frantic manner. It buzzed not once, but several times, and then, after a pause, more times again.

Henri van der Vreken ran upstairs and entered his employer's bedroom. The lights were on. The room, usually as neat as a pin, was in a state of shambles, as if a violent struggle had taken place. The twin beds were pushed askew. Between them, on the floor, lay Tarnower. Dressed in his beige-colored pajamas, he was flat on his back. There was blood all over his night clothes, the bedspread, and on the floor.

As van der Vreken stared in shock, Tarnower revived momentarily. He saw van der Vreken, and opened his mouth to try to say something to him. Van der Vreken leaned down, but Tarnower was unable to get any words out. He fell back, unconscious.

In moments Suzanne van der Vreken was calling the police from a downstairs telephone. It was later discovered that the telephone in Tarnower's bedroom was inoperative. Suzanne van Vreken was not able to speak English very well, but she did manage to let the White Plains police know that there was trouble at the Tarnower house. The call was logged as the report of a burglary.

White Plains police relayed the information immediately to the Harrison Town Police. Sergeant John Carney, the desk officer, called Harrison Patrolman Brian McKenna to investigate. McKenna sped toward the Tarnower house in the driving rain.

There are no numbers on Purchase Street, which runs about ten miles from Rye, New York, to the Old Post Road near the Kensico Reservoir, but there is a telephone pole with a red "T" painted on one side in front of the Tarnower estate.

McKenna found it without difficulty.

There is some confusion over exactly what happened when McKenna got to the Tarnower home and turned in at the five-hundred-foot driveway. At least five different versions appeared in the newspapers on March 12. A reconstructed version of what probably happened follows.

As the patrol car turned in at the driveway and started up the road toward the house, McKenna glanced in his rear-view mirror and saw the headlights of a car following him. When he stopped in front of the big house, a blue Chrysler sedan pulled up behind him and stopped.

A woman rolled down the window on the driver's side. She leaned her head out of the car into the rain and turned off the engine.

"There's been a shooting," she said, as it was reported later. "I think I have killed Hi."

McKenna jumped immediately out of the patrol car and ran up the steps to the front door, which opened for him. The van der Vrekens were waiting; they took him upstairs to the master bedroom. Behind him, the woman who had been in the car got out and climbed the front steps in the downpour.

In the bedroom McKenna saw that Tarnower was unconscious and bleeding from what appeared to be bullet wounds. Immediately he tried to keep Tarnower alive with CPR (cardiopulmonary resuscitation). As he worked, he was able to use his walkie-talkie to summon an ambulance and backup officers.

In a few minutes the ambulance arrived. The attendant took one look at Tarnower, and he and the driver rolled Tarnower onto a portable stretcher and carried him downstairs. Then they were off to St. Agnes Hospital in White Plains, where, ironically enough, Tarnower was a consulting cardiologist.

Meanwhile, two more Harrison police officers arrived at the house. They were Daniel O'Sullivan and Arthur Siciliano. As they got out of their patrol car and ran up the steps to the front door of the Tarnower house, they were met by the woman standing there in the doorway, drenched now by the rain. She might have been waiting for them to arrive.

Blonde and in her fifties, she was slightly built, and dressed in tan slacks, with a dark mink jacket that looked quite expensive slung over her shoulders. She was soaked. She was a good-looking, coolly elegant woman, one who the officers knew was used to deferential treatment. The only jarring note in her appearance was a swelling on her upper lip which appeared to have been bruised and a discoloration on her face near her right eye.

"Dr. Tarnower has been shot," she told them. Then she added, abruptly, and with a tremor of emotion, as the officers said later, "I shot him. I did it."

She then told them that she was Mrs. Jean Struven Harris. At this point, Siciliano reportedly gave her the set speech advising her of her constitutional rights, and she immediately

21

assented that she understood.

One of the officers asked her where she had left the gun.

She told them that she did not have the gun with her but had taken it out of the bedroom and had put it in her car.

In the glove compartment of the Chrysler, O'Sullivan found a .32 caliber Harrington & Richardson revolver packed in a box. It had been broken—that is, the cylinder containing the bullets had been removed from the frame. There was blood on the metal surface.

She told the two officers that she had driven to New York from Virginia that evening. "I wanted Dr. Tarnower to kill me," it was reported she said. "I had no intention of ever going back to Virginia alive."

Later she told them that she had left notes back in her home in Virginia explaining why she was going to do what she had done—although it had not turned out the way she had expected.

The officers asked her to describe what had happened in the bedroom. First she told them, according to their report, that she had parked in front of the house and had entered it through the garage. It was a familiar entryway for her, since she had come to the house many times to be with Tarnower.

She had not disturbed the housekeeping couple and had walked right upstairs to Tarnower's bedroom. Briefly, she explained that the two of them had begun to argue.

Although her explanation was somewhat disjointed and was difficult to follow, she said they were arguing about their relationship. She told the police that she had brought the gun that they had found along with her so that Tarnower could finish the job he had started on her.

He had ruined her life, she said. She had been in love with him for many years, and she thought he loved her. But he kept going out with other women.

"He slept with every woman he could," she said at one point, according to the report filed later.

Because he wouldn't marry her, he was ruining her life. She said she was unable to work because she was upset, thinking about him. He had made it impossible for her to be what she was—a professional teacher and headmistress. How could she on when he would not marry her?

She was living a lie. No one could live a lie and teach young girls to be honest and fine. She was a moral and decent woman—but she could not live a moral and decent life unless he married her.

She wanted him to take the gun and kill her—finish what he had started to do already.

During the fight, as reported in the *Daily News*, she said, Tarnower had shouted at her, "Get out of here, you're crazy!"

But she would not leave. Apparently she persisted. He must have tried to push her away and get her out of his bedroom. He started to hit her.

He was a strong man, and he apparently bruised her on the eye and on the lip. But she continued to plead with him to kill her.

She told police she couldn't remember the details of all the struggle. Then suddenly, shots were fired.

Siciliano asked her who had pulled the trigger.

Apparently forgetting that she had already said she had shot him, she murmured: "I don't know."

"What happened then?" O'Sullivan asked.

She told them that she had thrown the gun in the bathtub. That didn't make much sense. They had found the gun in the glove compartment of the car. How had it got from the bathtub to the car?

Jean Harris never explained.

There was more, but nothing that could give a more accurate picture of what had happened in the bedroom.

The officers finally took her to the Harrison police station for further questioning. The interrogation lasted several hours.

The possible confusion in the preceding sequence of events stems from the fact that there are at least five different versions about exactly what did happen when Officer McKenna drove up toward the Tarnower house after being dispatched there to look into a possible burglary.

One version—that which appeared on the Associated Press wires under the byline of Eileen Putnam—said:

"Mrs. Harris . . . was arrested as she backed a car out of a long driveway to the house . . . ."

The *Washington Post*, in a story assembled from news services, said: "Harris was discovered by police as she backed out of Tarnower's driveway. . . ."

The *New York Daily News,* in a story bylined by John Randazzo, Jesse Brodey and Brian Kates, said:

"Officer Brian McKenna . . . stopped Harris

as she was driving away from the house."
Another sentence said: "Harris was picked up
by police later Monday as she was leaving Tarnower's . . . home."

The *New York Post*, in a story by Cy Egan,
said: ". . . McKenna raced to the home in time
to see Mrs. Harris' 1973 Chrysler sedan leaving
the driveway. At the sight of the flashing lights
of his radio car, Mrs. Harris made a U-turn and
reentered the driveway."

James Feron, in a special to the *New York
Times,* quoted the police report itself, which
said:

"[McKenna] met a vehicle exiting the Tarnower driveway, with a woman operator, later
identified as Jean Harris."

Feron's story continued:

"Officer McKenna, the lights on his patrolcar
flashing, said the other car made a U-turn and
re-entered the driveway. The officer raced past
her and up the stairs to Dr. Tarnower's bedroom. . . ."

The point is obvious: if, as the press reported,
Jean Harris was leaving the house and was
"stopped" and "picked up" or "arrested," or
"discovered" by the police, she might have been
trying to escape from the vicinity of the Tarnower house. In turn, this would make it appear
as if she might be trying to put as much distance
between herself and the Tarnower house as she
could, possibly to escape involvement in what
had occurred there.

But, if she passed McKenna in the police car
and then turned around and came back, she
might have been trying to seek help for Tarnower. And that would bear out a point later

made by her attorney, Joel Aurnou, who said that "the phone in Dr. Tarnower's room did not work," and that she was driving to a phone to call police when they arrived. According to Aurnou, the police "also were unable to use [the phone] later." The telephone on which the housekeeper had made the call to the police was on a separate line.

The police interrogation involved a number of other statements that did not come out until a preliminary hearing was held some three days later.

Meanwhile, at St. Agnes Hospital, where Tarnower had been taken in the ambulance, he was fighting for his life. Desperate efforts were being made by his colleagues in medicine to save him.

He had been hit four times by bullets that had come from the blood-stained .32 caliber Harrington & Richardson revolver that had been taken out of the box in Harris' glove compartment and given to police.

One bullet had gone through his right hand, entering from the palm. Another had struck his right arm in the upper arm. A third had hit him in the upper chest on the right-hand side, just below the right shoulder. The fourth bullet had entered his body from the rear; the point of entry was also on his right-hand side, quite near the spine.

All the medical help in the world would have been to no avail. Within an hour of the shooting, sometime near midnight, Tarnower died.

Jean Harris was charged with second-degree murder and held in the Westchester County jail without bail.

2

The Victim

Herman Tarnower was born on March 18, 1910, in Brooklyn, New York. His father, Harry Tarnower, was an affluent New York hat manufacturer. There were four children in the family—three girls and a boy.

The boy grew up in a household in which one did the "right thing" at the "right time," in which there was always good food to eat, in which manners were stressed at meal times, in which one ate slowly and calmly, enjoying conversation and comfort at the table.

In fact, food was one of the very important matters in the Tarnower household. Although the Tarnowers were well-to-do, the young boy's mother, Dora Tarnower, was an excellent cook. She instilled in all her children an avid interest in the best of foods.

She was, in the opinion of many, a "fine" cook. She excelled particularly in exotic dishes. Her menus were based mostly on Russian and Turkish cuisine. Later on in his life, when his love of good food had been firmly established, he would recall that she concentrated mostly on a large number of marinated meat dishes, particularly lamb, and that her cabbage and sauerkraut soup was an unforgettable event in the lives of the young Tarnowers.

Food, while one of the highlights of the young boy's life, was not the be-all and end-all of his existence. He was in many ways a normal boy who exercised and ran about like all other boys, building his muscles and playing with his friends.

But his affluence made him different from some of his peers. While others of his generation were reduced to rushing about in the streets of Brooklyn trying to scrape up an extra penny here and there to help out with the finances, Herman sat home reading the classics, studying his school work, and in general learning to acclimate himself to live the life of the well-to-do.

From the beginning, he excelled at scholarship. Because his family believed that a man with brains should become a professional, it was always understood from the first that Herman Tarnower, if at all possible, would become a doctor when he grew up. Everything he did from his early years prepared him for that profession.

There was never any question but that he would succeed. If he chanced to fail at his chosen profession, he would certainly succeed at something equally as lucrative. He was bright, if not brilliant, and he was inculcated from birth with the desire to succeed and to overcome all obstacles that might be in his way.

Money was never a problem in the Tarnower family, nor was the easy sociability of the affluent and successful. The Tarnowers were people who loved the trappings of culture, and were determined to live the "good life."

Some of his peers might laugh at him, but Herman Tarnower grew up understanding the intellectual life and reveling in it. He had a quick

28

mind, a quick wit, and a comprehension and perception that outdistanced that of most of his friends and neighbors. Nevertheless, his parents did not let his precocious intelligence go to his head. They kept him always aware that he must not rest on his laurels but keep pushing and always excel.

Which he did, with gusto.

Problem-solving was his metier. His mind was such that he could analyze a problem, strip it of its nonessentials, synthesize a solution, and prepare an answer that was not only accurate, but practical as well. He was never one to let minor inconveniences fog his mind or prevent him from seeing the correct and most practical solution to any problem almost instantly.

In spite of his absorption with the academic side of life, he was a balanced man. He was lean and angular, and his sinews were tough. He was not afraid of pain. He was quick and his reflexes were excellent. He kept in trim even when he was small. Those were years when Teddy Roosevelt's philosophy of the healthy mind in the healthy body was accepted throughout America as the gospel. He loved sports: he would play as much as possible with the kids on the block.

As he grew up through adolescence, Herman Tarnower was the pride of his parents. Even though he was one of four children, the fact that he was male gave him some preferential treatment during those formative years.

When he had attained his full growth he was over six feet in height, with a tough, lean frame that did not easily put on fat. He liked to watch teamwork sports like basketball and football. But he was actively fascinated with individual sports like hunting and fishing.

From his youth on he read books on exotic locales like Africa and Australia. He had read books by Theodore Roosevelt on big-game hunting. His dream was to go on safari in Africa and bag a lion or two!

He was equally interested in his own manhood. As the only boy in a family of three sisters, he found himself more and more turning into what we would now call a "macho" personality. His family background was such that his father—the man—was definitely and without question the head of the family. The women were subservient to the men. That was the family pattern.

Herman Tarnower thought it was a mighty fine way to live.

By the time he was in college at Syracuse, he was being called by the nickname "Hi"—whether because of his height, or his name "Herman," or a combination of both really isn't known.

College was a breeze for him. The intellectual life was his natural milieu. He liked the conviviality of campus life. He liked the companionship of people who were his mental equals.

Irving Pasternack, who attended the university with Tarnower, remembered him as having been polite and intelligent during his college years. He always had a serious appearance.

"He was a member of Phi Epsilon Pi fraternity, one of the wealthier and more prestigious fraternities on the campus, an ivy-covered Tudor-style mansion, where, however, he didn't live," Pasternack recalled.

Tarnower lived off campus in an apartment he

rented. He had bought—a rare thing even in those days before the Depression—and "drove around in . . . a two-seater sports car."

In fact, it was Tarnower's success at Syracuse that actually got Pasternack to go there. Irving's mother was a representative for the university who would meet with prospective students. She was so taken with Tarnower that she told her son, "If that's what they produce at Syracuse, you have to go."

And Pasternack enrolled the following autumn. It was then that he formed a friendship with Tarnower.

"While other guys were trying to crack marks of C, Tarnower was always cracking A's. He was always studying."

Tarnower dressed conservatively, as might be imagined from his haberdashery-conscious background in Brooklyn. His clothes were good ones, however. On campus he appeared as a distinguished type, "confident, quiet and withdrawn." Pasternack said he was a "quiet man" who didn't hang around the fraternity house like the other members did.

The wife of another classmate of Tarnower at Syracuse saw him in a different light. "He was a cool cucumber," she said. "He didn't relate to women."

There were contradictions, obviously, in Tarnower—even at that formative age. But if he was stand-offish, he was not stand-offish through fear or insecurity. He knew what he was good at, and he knew he was going to get what he wanted from college.

Those who attended university in the late

31

1920s were a select few—quite unlike the collegian of today. Hi Tarnower knew he was one of those destined to make it big in the world. He had the brains, he had the shrewdness, he had the personality to succeed at anything he attempted.

And he was right.

In 1933 he received his Medical Degree from Syracuse University. It was an inauspicious year, any way one looked at it. The Stock Market crash had occurred in 1929. Some intimates of the Tarnowers had committeed suicide, and others were standing in bread lines, but the Tarnower luck seemed to hold.

Hi Tarnower was not really concerned too much with the problems of the out-of-work or the unlucky. Shrewd, he knew exactly what to do to make his life good.

During the depths of the Great Depression, he did his internship and residency in internal medicine at Bellevue Hospital in New York. Everywhere around him the Great American Dream was falling apart. In addition to breadlines across the length and breadth of the land, there were marches on government institutions. There were strikes in effect everywhere. It was the worst of times—all over the world.

Hi Tarnower exulted in the challenge.

Even medicine was changing in those bleak years. Since the early days of the republic, the typical physician had been the "general practitioner," the G.P., the Marcus Welby with a black satchel, the kindly gentleman who came around to the house and popped pills into the mouths of men, women and children.

But along about the turn of the Twentieth

Century, things were beginning to change in medicine. The General Practitioner, although he did not know it, was actually on his way out. The practice of medicine was not general any longer, but was beginning to fragment into "specialties."

In the 1800s, the physician received his medical degree, hung out his shingle, and went into practice as a G.P. But in the 1930s, many things were changing. Because of the complexity of new drugs, new equipment, new techniques, more and more individuals were branching out into specialties like surgery, eye, ear, nose and throat, orthopedics, and so on.

New specialties were springing up everywhere. One of the newest was a little-known and little-recognized splinter practice called cardiology. Deaths from heart disease were at an all-time high in the 1930s—possibly due to emotional stress caused by the Depression and its attendant pressures.

Tarnower had made his mind up years before to study internal medicine and perhaps to be a general practitioner. Howerver, with things in medicine changing so rapidly, he decided to look around a bit before settling down as an old-fashioned door-to-door doctor.

While he was waiting to make up his mind, he opened up an office as a general practitioner in New York City. He practiced in the office for a few years, becoming accustomed to the routine and thriving on it. He had always liked people—and he learned that he enjoyed keeping them healthy.

But his mind was open, his interests wide. Simply dishing out pills soon palled on him. It

33

just wasn't his idea of a good medical practice. With his restless intellect, he began casting around for some more demanding type of practice.

In 1936 he was awarded the Bowen Fellowship by the New York Academy of Medicine. The Fellowship enabled him to travel abroad and study medical advances in Europe. He leaped at the opportunity to explore new possibilities in medicine.

His studies took him to England and Holland. He was fascinated by London, and loved being there. He made the acquaintance of a number of other physicians, and learned all he could about European medicine. What he didn't like he quickly discarded; what he did like he quickly assimilated.

After London, he went to Holland, and while there picked up the rudiments of the Dutch language. Years later, when he moved to Purchase, he hired a Belgian-French couple to work for him. He had always liked European cuisine and the Continental manner of living.

By the time he had finished with the Fellowship, he had just about decided on going into cardiology. As a new specialty it was a challenge, and the study of the heart appealed to him. So many people he knew had relatives who had died of heart disease. In a way, it was almost like the Twentieth Century version of the Black Plague.

When he returned to the United States in 1938, he did not go back to New York City. Instead he moved out into the suburbs, to a small, very posh, influential settlement called Scarsdale. So many well-to-do people lived in Scarsdale that the name had become synonymous with luxury and wealth.

Grasslands Hospital, located in Valhalla, New York, did not have a cardiology department, but wanted to, start one. Tarnower was hired to establish the department and become its director of cardiology. [Grasslands eventually changed its name to Westchester General Hospital.]

His offices were located in an apartment building in the middle of town. He lived there too. For a number of years he seemed to thrive as a rising young doctor.

In short order he became attending cardiologist at White Plains Hospital, situated near Scarsdale and Valhalla, and also an assistant physician at Presbyterian Hospital in New York City.

Although the practice of cardiology was growing by leaps and bounds, there was little even at that time that a doctor could do for cardiac cases except treat them as best he could. Sedated bedrest was the primary recommendation for victims. While most of Dr. Tarnower's experiences during those beginning years involved the practice of medicine on a family level, he was learning a great deal about the heart and how it functioned. He was also learning how the heart became overtaxed—especially by excessive weight and emotional stress.

While he learned, he earned. He was making money, as they used to say, "hand over fist." He was a dynamic and charming man with a magnetic personality that drew people to him. His appeal was especially effective on susceptible women—and there were plenty of Scarsdale wives around who could have felt susceptible to him. Those were the days when most wives did not work; many of the suburban wives had live-in help and were very bored with their easy lives. Tarnower was not a boring man.

He made no bones about the fact that he was a man of very demanding appetites for the better things in life—and that included high cuisine, high art, high society. It also most especially included the society of beautiful, compelling, and willing women.

His personal taste grew more and more impeccable as his professional life flourished. Scarsdale was at that time as important as Beverly Hills as a nucleus of the most beautiful, most daring, and most stimulating women in the country. The richest and most prestigious individuals in the New York milieu were escaping to the suburbs at that time. The poshest of those suburbs was located right around Hi Tarnower's doorstep.

Even with the Great Depression persisting into the late 1930s, Tarnower's income rose rapidly. He began accumulating art treasures and other acquisitions that seemed to satisfy his growing taste for the sybaritic lifestyle. And his palate was becoming sharpened by his acquaintance-ship with patients and friends who were wealthy and highly placed in society.

Yet there was a cloud on the horizon. Europe was already in the midst of a devastating war which was blowing the continent apart. England was now in it, London torn to pieces by German air raids. It was only a matter of time before the U.S. got into the war—but the people and Congress weren't about to let that happen without a struggle.

When war started, it didn't begin in Europe at

all, but in a totally unexpected place: right on America's back doorstep, in Honolulu. When Pearl Harbor was bombed, it wasn't long before Tarnower offered his services to Uncle Sam. He was commissioned as a medical corps officer to serve in the United States Army Air Corps —which soon became the U.S. Army Air Force, and later, the U.S. Air Force.

He served out his time during World War II at various hospital bases. He took to the military life like a duck to water. His asceticism, his dry intellectual wit, his ability to concentrate on one goal and succeed made him the perfect military man.

He was tall, and still slender. The military strictures of posture, obedience and conviction were right down his alley. He became the super-military officer. It had always been in him, but it took the military life to bring it out where it showed.

"He was an autocrat," said one colleague, "with a military bearing, someone very firm in opinion."

"He was a perfectionist," another brief acquaintance said. "He was used to being in charge, used to people snapping to attention. Your typical chief-of-staff, humorless, not given to small talk. A very private human being."

The innate ability to put everything out of his mind but the primary objective made Dr. Tarnower a formidable person. Basically, he was a natural leader of men. His intellect was fine-tuned, his inhibitions few, and he had no sentimentality that might cloud his judgment.

"He was a leader, thoroughly masculine," said a close friend of Tarnower's later, reflecting the truth about Tarnower in those war years.

A photograph of Tarnower in his uniform of Major in the Medical Corps attached to the Army Air Corps shows a stern-faced, unsmiling, resolute face representing total strength, durability, and unflinching austerity.

His record in the armed services must have been an excellent one. In 1945, at the close of the war, Tarnower received a call from General Douglas MacArthur. MacArthur gave him a real plum of an assignment. He was appointed as a member of the Atomic Bomb Casualty Survey Commission. It was this commission that went into Nagasaki and Hiroshima and studied the devastation wreaked on the cities after the dropping of the world's first two A-Bombs. The study was made by both American and Japanese teams.

"It was the most significant and important experience in my entire medical career," Tarnower said later. The study made a deep impression on him. He came back home convinced that there should be no more wars, that people should be allowed to talk out their differences, that everyone was endowed from the beginning with the right to live. This was the humane aspect of his essentially autocratic personality.

Upon his return to civilian life, he tried to pick up his practice—and his life—where he had left it. In addition to his work at Grasslands, White Plains, and Presbyterian, N.Y., he also became a consulting cardiologist at St. Agnes Hospital in White Plains.

His service in the armed forces had revived his interest in the outdoor life. In a few years, air travel had shrunk the world to a much smaller place, and he began indulging himself in his favorite longtime dream—big-game hunting. He flew down to Africa, and became a safari hunter.

Hunting game was only one part of his wide participation in sports. He also alternated trips to Iceland and Scotland to fly-fish for salmon. In addition to these exotic and expensive pursuits, he continued his favorite exercise: golf. He played regularly at the Century Country Club in Westchester County close to the Connecticut border.

It was during those days that he conceived a lasting affection for the lovely terrain surrounding the golf course. If he ever had a home, he decided, he would have it right around that part of Westchester.

During the late 1940s and 1950s, Tarnower was living and practicing in a small, tastefully furnished apartment in Scarsdale. Now he wanted more room. Even though he was still a bachelor, he wanted a place to rattle around in. He had the money, and he had the place in mind. He had only to select a particular spot to buy.

It was on the golf course that he finally decided he would not purchase a home in that part of Westchester County, but would *build* one to his own liking.

By now he had been around the world many times, traveling almost anywhere his fancy took him. Of all the places he went, he was most impressed by Japan. He had fought the Japanese during World War II, but he had seen what the A-Bomb did to Nagasaki and Hiroshima, and how Japan had responded to this challenge. The country had come back to be one of the most dynamic economic powers in the world.

Tarnower was fascinated by the religion, and by the art and architecture, as well as the lifestyle of the people. The Japanese were civilized, polished, and intelligent. He was impressed by their social mores—their bathing together, both sexes mixed, their ability to co-habit with one another without the petty jealousies and bickering so characteristic of the average American family.

Tarnower hired an architect and had his house built to his own design specifications—a Japanese-type modern structure located on a rolling hillside.

"He was hung up on Buddhas and Buddha sculpture," said sculptor Harry Hauptman of Scarsdale. Hauptman was a patient of Tarnower's who had gone to him with a heart problem.

Tarnower asked Hauptman to create a Buddha sculpture for his estate. But before he could finish it Tarnower found a concrete one in China, and Hauptman lost the commission.

"He was a marvelous cardiologist," Hauptman said. "Very capable, confidence-inspiring. When he advised something you did it without hesitation. Very few patients ever sought a second opinion."

When the house on Purchase Street was finished, Tarnower added a swimming pool and a tennis court at the rear of the property.

In the house he now displayed is most rewarding collection: the heads of his big game trophies, mounted and hung in one of the rooms along with the art treasures he had been collecting for years.

It was the next year, 1959, that he decided he would branch out professionally as well as personally.

He had observed the success of the West Coast idea of the medical "clinic"—a grouping together of several medical practices linked in complementary fashion usually under one roof. Tarnower conceived the Scarsdale Medical Group, operating out of the Scarsdale Medical Center. He was the guiding hand that got it off the ground, and who owned its property, structure, and appurtenances.

There was already in existence an incipient "clinic"—two doctors who had banded together to share office space in the Thornycroft Apartments on Garth Road. Tarnower went to them, told them he had an idea for a medical center, explained what he wanted, and convinced them that it was a good idea.

Another doctor was invited to the group, and the four of them became the Scarsdale Medical Group.

Even the Center's physical properties show Tarnower's obvious influence. The building has a modern design quite reminiscent of Tarnower's own home. He built it flat and low-lying, with a great deal of glass on the exterior. Inside, the ceilings have high rafters.

From the beginning, the Scarsdale Medical Center was a tremendous success. It was staffed at first by the four doctors who founded it. At the end of twenty-one years, there were nine internists affiliated with the Center. Tarnower knew exactly what to do to bring the practice of medicine to the Westchester County suburbs.

In the early 1960s, the suburbs around Westchester were burgeoning with rich young couples and their children. It was also crammed with hard-working executives approaching retirement age and their well-fed wives—both prime targets for cardiac arrest.

It was alright to be comfortably well-off, but it was not alright to be too well-fed. In Tarnower's judgment, it was simply foolish to overeat and endanger one's health by putting on too much girth.

There was one way to avoid overweight: by dieting.

Shortly after opening the clinic, Tarnower began working out a diet that would appeal to the affluent and luxury-loving men and women who were his patients. He knew their tastes differed from that of the average population because of their acquaintance with gourmet foods. He knew they would relapse into overeating once they finished a diet, only to gain back all the lost weight.

The problem, as he saw it, was to devise a regimen of dieting that not only kept calories at a minimum, but tasted good as well. In other words, along with a strict regimen that would keep their intake within the proper parameters, he would achieve a balance that would keep the pounds off and cut down on the obvious strain on the heart.

The diet he dreamed up became the Scarsdale Diet.

Professionally, Tarnower was widening his horizons. From 1957 to 1962, he was associate professor of clinical rehabilitation medicine at New York University, and clinical professor at

New York Medical College. In 1950 he helped found the Westchester County Chapter of the American Heart Association. From 1950 to 1951 he served as its president.

He continued filling his house with big game trophies—but he had yet to fill it with a wife. When his friends kidded him about the fact that he was a bachelor—and at the age of 50 years!—he would laugh and remark:

"I'm too busy with the practice of medicine to get around to it."

But that wasn't quite the truth. He was not too busy to be a very companionable man, easy in social situations, attractive to women, and a good date. Too busy to marry? He was, truly, the typical "swinging bachelor" of the era—at the same time a man who remained essentially an extremely private person. When he swung, no one but the person he was swinging with knew it.

Of course, there were rumors.

His romantic life continued to be, as always, "prodigious," as *People Magazine* wrote in a piece on him. Often Tarnower's "dates" were widows, unmarried young ladies, or divorcées. Although some women considered him "austere" and "aloof," even "cold," others did not.

"He looks like a lizard," one of them said of him, "but he's got charm enough to talk the birds down out of the trees!"

It was true. He was *not* a physically prepossessing man at all. In the 1970s he was in his sixties—sporting some white hair on top of his head, but still that trim lean figure.

There was a vibrancy in him, a challenging vitality that swept everything before it. He had such a sense of self-possession that he could charm anyone he wanted to. And the women, even if they might be a bit put off by his personal appearance and his age, soon realized that it bothered them not at all.

He was a hard man to reject or ignore.

Not only his patients but those who worked for him and around him were all fair game. He chose with discretion and with such consummate taste that there were never any embarrassing repercussions.

He had style. He had class. He was a cultured, appreciative man, a man accustomed to assuming just the proper bonhomie, the right attitude, the proper panache to bring it all off.

He preferred to be with the affluent. After all, he had been born to the purple. He appreciated the civilized. Because people who did not grow up with money were apt to be reverse snobs, he did not particularly like to associate socially with them. His own sisters had married well, and were bringing up children whom Tarnower liked and approved of.

If his bachelorhood ever seemed a problem to him, he never mentioned it. He attacked that situation like any one of his many problems. In analyzing it, he quite probably reasoned that he was indeed wedded to his work rather than to a wife. But since he needed female companionship as a normal outlet for his emotions, he preferred the untangled relationship he would get from casual acquaintances rather than a permanent bond like marriage.

He liked variety in art, in big game, *and* his women. They were all pursuits which he followed with avid excitement. They kept him in trim.

44

They kept his vital juices flowing. If he were to marry, he would probably miss the fun of the quest.

Whatever his reasoning, he had decided long ago that he would never marry. And to his dying day, he never did.

The rumors abounded about his exploits. He never made the mistake of pursuing a woman who was too much for him. Nor did he ever really pursue one who was totally uninterested in him. He selected with care, and weighed the game carefully before pouncing.

Once he landed his trophy, he could be merciless if she did not measure up to his preconceived and extremely high standards. One tale that surfaced during his last weeks was of a woman whom he met in the Caribbean during a trip. He invited her on a round-the-world tour with him. She was eager to accept and they departed on schedule.

However, in the middle of the globe-trotting voyage, something happened. No one really knows what—including perhaps, even the lady involved. Whatever it was, Tarnower soured on her, and immediately dropped her, according to the story, like the proverbial "hot potato."

That was, according to reports, at the midway point of the world tour. When she protested, he reportedly "roughed her up before he left."

The next thing she knew, Tarnower had departed the tour, and had vanished.

Humiliated but unable to strike back at him in his absence, she stuck out the tour to the bitter end, but she never saw the doctor again. No one took Tarnower to task. Actually, he was said to have then joined a "divorcée" who was one of his assistants at his Scarsdale Medical Center.

According to the story, he took her off to the very Caribbean Island where he had met his globe-trotting companion, even "whisked [her] to the home of the woman he'd deserted."

There were other examples. It was said he had a negative side to his personality that matched perfectly in mirror reverse his charm and intellectual suavity. He had been known to blow up verbally at a companion, and, after subjecting her to humiliating verbal abuse, would begin slapping her around and assaulting her physically.

No one ever took him up on this. No one ever specifically accused him of assault. But it was rumored that he could be mean and vindictive when he felt crossed, betrayed, or even insulted.

Most of the time he was easy-going, surface-smooth, and polished. Most of the time he was the debonair sybarite, the hedonist with all the social graces.

And he did, after all, have one especially favorite companion during the last fourteen years of his life.

Her name was Jean Struven Harris.

They traveled all over the globe, eating in restaurants, living in hotels, for weeks at a time, obviously liked the same things, hated the same things, were almost the same as a wedded couple.

It was a strange relationship: he, a laidback male, a swinging bachelor, a man without pretensions to marriage. She, a moralistic, almost prim blueblood, who wanted marriage, permanence, and marriage above all else. From the beginning the relationship was doomed to fail.

And fail it did, eventually, in a particularly grisly and melodramatic manner. But before it failed, there were warning beacons all along the way that should have alerted both Hi Tarnower and Jean Harris that they were on a collision course and that the only possible conclusion would be violence.

Both chose to ignore the warning signals. Each chose to believe in qualities in the other that simply did not exist. Each considered the other to be guided by the same precepts of behavior and lifestyle. Both considered themselves aware of any dangers that might exist in the relationship that developed.

Both were wrong—tragically so.

How did the trouble start?

What really went wrong?

Why did it all end in bloodshed, ruin, and death?

3

The Headmistress (I)

Jean Witte Struven was born in Cleveland, Ohio, during the early part of the decade this country has called "the roaring twenties." Her father was a career military officer, a career which in those days allowed a man to live the life of the affluent middle class.

Like Hi Tarnower, Jean Struven was born into affluence, and, if not into great wealth, at least into an atmosphere that embodied all the virtues of a life of luxury.

She grew up in Shaker Heights, Cleveland's wealthy suburb, where she was friendly with the sons and daughters of the rich, respected, and privileged. Although her formative years carried on through the days of the Great Depression, she, like Hi Tarnower, was little affected by the povery, the panic, the lack of money that turned the country into a land of desperation and despair.

Neither she nor her two sisters or brother were much affected by the economic disaster or by any of its manifold complicated incidents, or aftermaths.

Struven went to grammar school in Roxboro Elementary School in Cleveland. A classmate who attended Roxboro once said of her, "She was a fine, wonderful girl, and a leader."

Through her high school years, she was enrolled in Laurel School for Girls, in Shaker Heights, one of the best of the exclusive private schools for women in the country. There she grew up with and learned with Cleveland's best.

She was a good student—in fact, an excellent one—who accepted the rigors of her private-school environment without quarrel, resentment, or resistance. From the beginning, she fit in. She liked the female camaraderie, the precepts of life, the convictions that the teachers espoused.

And, from the beginning, Struven was an achiever. In her senior year she was elected president of the senior class at Laurel, and soon after that, graduated with honors from the prestigious school.

Having acquired the proper polish for the well-brought-up young lady of the 1930s, she applied for enrollment at Smith College in Northampton, Massachusetts, and was accepted without hesitation—her background at Laurel obviously having helped her through the usual admissions-office hurdles.

From 1941 through 1945 she studied history and economics at Smith. Those were the years of World War II—from Pearl Harbor, December 7, 1941, to Hiroshima, 1945. "We gave our bicycles to the Waves and our blood to the Red Cross," her class wrote in the 1945 Smith yearbook. In spite of the mention of the war, she was insulated from its effects on campus, even though she was as "involved" as anyone.

At Smith she impressed her teachers and fellow students with her intelligence, diligence, and basic orientation to the work ethic. Although she did engage occasionally in typical campus hi-jinks, she was really a hard-working and industrious student rather than a playgirl.

"I lived across the hall from her," said one friend. "She was a terribly fine person, well-ordered, so in control of her life."

She was in enough control, even in those hectic years, to graduate magna cum laude from Smith in 1945 with a B.A. in economics. But she had not spent all her time at Smith cracking the books. She had some time for a social life.

In May, 1946, she married James S. Harris, the son of a socially prominent Grosse Pointe, Michigan, family. Harris was the epitome of the "tall, dark, and handsome" suitor so sought after by nubile women in those days. And he was rich and smooth as well.

The Harrises settled in Grosse Pointe Farm, a settlement of small homes for young couples, where they lived in a four-bedroom colonial rambler.

In the fall of 1946, Jean Harris went to work at the Grosse Pointe Country Day School as a teacher of history and current events—two subjects she had concentrated on and done so well in at Smith. She worked there for four years, when she suddenly quit her job to raise a family.

Her first son, David, was born in 1950. Two years later her second son, James Jr., was born.

Meanwhile, her husband had taken a job as supervisor at the Holly Carburetor Company outside Detroit. Jean Harris spent those years at home, taking care of her young offspring.

By 1954, she decided that she had brought the boys up past the critical stages of their baby years and decided to go back to work.

One report has it that she started a nursery school to teach the young children in the area, but that after a few months of operation she closed it down. Whether it was because the school was not drawing enough pupils or because she received a job offer is not clear. But she did get a job offer from Grosse Pointe Country Day School.

There was a teacher vacancy in the first grade, and Jean Harris became a first-grade teacher. "She was a very good teacher, very well liked, a very fine person," said the secretary to the school's headmaster.

According to another source, Jean Harris displayed an impatience with any of her colleagues "who didn't measure up."

It apparently never occurred to Jean Harris that her own extreme competency was an unusual thing. She seemed to expect the same efficiency and intelligence from everyone around her. When she did not get it, she tended to become upset.

She set extremely high standards for herself, said one of her colleagues there, and expected others to achieve the same excellence. She also had the faculty of setting a goal for herself and inexorably pursuing that goal until she had achieved it. And she seemed not to be able to understand why everyone couldn't succeed just as easily.

But she had other qualities that were obvious and that did not bother others as much as her extreme competence.

"She was very attractive," recalled the director of the lower school. "A very pretty woman, who was able to handle both family and school life. She did a lot of writing for the school publications."

In spite of her outward appearance of calm and control, Jean Harris was restless. Her life was a good one—she had both family and career at a time when not every wife could afford to have both—but she felt that she was missing something.

It was said that she tried to persuade her husband to travel with her, but he was apparently so busy with his job that he couldn't find the time. In 1958, Jean Harris took a long trip to Russia, which was just opening up for travel, and toured the area around Moscow briefly.

When she returned, she lectured to the school of her trip. Everyone was impressed by her ability to accomplish what she set out to do. No one knew it at the time, but she was hoping to become assistant to the director of Grosse Pointe Country Day School.

She did not get the appointment. Her ambition of which not everyone was aware had been thwarted, and surely she had become upset. Her friends at the school may have been aware she was having family troubles at the same time that she was having professional troubles. Since, however, she never confided in anyone, her emotions could have seethed within her.

Bertram Shover, director of the lower school at Grosse Pointe Country Day School, recalled: "Very few personal matters did she ever bring up. She was ambitious and she wanted to promote herself."

Whatever her emotional problems were, on October 24, 1964, she filed for a divorce, asking for the Grosse Pointe Farms home, and custody of the two children. She charged her husband with "extreme and repeated cruelty," in the legal jargon of the day.

James Harris agreed to the terms of the divorce, but he also claimed that she was guilty of "cruelty" also. Within a few months the divorce went through, and in March 1965, they were separated. James Harris was ordered to pay $27 a week in child support for each of his sons.

Shortly after this, Jean Harris obtained a master's degree in education from Wayne State University. "She was a very bright, very goal-directed person," said Dr. Cynthia Colvin, her advisor at Wayne State.

In fact, Dr. Colvin advised her to continue a few more years and get a doctorate in education. Jean Harris may have been in an emotional depression after the failure of her marriage. She was apparently facing a financial problem in trying to support her two boys. Whether or not she sought help from her parents for that support is not known.

Her decision was to take it all on herself and get a job. In fact, it may well be that she was fed up with Michigan and wanted a change of scenery. She told her friends at Wayne State that she had opted not to continue her education and would go to work to support her children and herself.

She began casting around for a suitable job. Finally she got one—and it was far enough away from Grosse Pointe to erase the bad memories of Michigan—as director of the middle school at the Springside School for girls in Chestnut Hill, Philadelphia.

In September, 1966, she packed up all her belongings and moved to Chestnut Hill, where she purchased a home and settled down with her two boys.

There she almost immediately, and with little effort, became a familiar part of the Chestnut Hill social scene. Why should it have been difficult for her—a young, good-looking, well-spoken divorcée with two well-brought up sons?

Apparently the area suited her better than Grosse Pointe.

She was approaching forty now, a difficult age for many women, but not particularly difficult for Jean Harris. She had always been good-looking, with her blue eyes, her natural blond hair, and her slender but shapely frame, her long, attractive legs. And with her self-control and assurance, she presented an image of a cool and very with-it woman.

There were always eligible bachelors and unattached males who would have been happy to squire her about. Her demands for entertainment were not overwhelming. She was an excellent ornament at any social gathering. Soon she was on at least casual terms with the movers of the social set in Philadelphia.

It was apparently in Philadelphia, during those years of her early divorcée-hood, that she met Dr. Herman Tarnower. Tarnower was typical of the bachelors who liked to escort her to social affairs, to the theater, and even on occasional vacation jaunts and voyages.

In 1972 another change occured in the life of Jean Harris. She was offered the job of headmistress at the Thomas School in Rowayton, Connecticut, a private girls school which had become plagued by a high turnover of administrators. It was also afflicted by declining enrollment.

She accepted the job, packed up, and made the move.

Some members of the staff at Thomas School, felt Jean Harris was "not terribly popular," nor in any way an outstanding headmistress.

Some thought that she did not get along so well with the staff. She was very emotional, one acquaintance said, "which would seem to make her job of administering to the students more difficult."

Her conversations, sometimes sprinkled with emotional outbursts, startled others.

An acquaintance of Jean Harris's remembered her as a "haughty, elegant woman, with a magnificent speaking voice and a lovely vocabulary. She reminded me of an actress."

But there was underlying her polish and outward calm a lack of warmth that became even chillier when one tried to establish any kind of friendship with her.

One story that surfaced at Thomas School about Jean Harris involved an experience she had at a drugstore in Rowayton. Rowayton is a typical suburban Connecticut community inhabited by well-to-do New York commuters and retired individuals subsisting comfortably on fat portfolios of stocks and bonds.

Into one of its quiet, refined and obviously sedate drugstores Jean Harris strolled one afternoon to have a prescription refilled. The prescription, fittingly enough, had been written out by Hi Tarnower.

The druggist read the prescription, and told

her that he would be unable to refill it without the doctor's verification, since it involved drugs that were on a control list.

Jean Harris, the story went, couldn't understand what was happening. When the druggist carefully repeated his statement to her, she turned red in the face and blew up.

"Her voice rose and she began talking very loudly," the *Washington Post* reported. "It was most embarrassing."

Finally Jean Harris dialed the police. After a few moments they arrived at the drugstore.

She told them that she was having trouble getting a legitimate prescription refilled and that the druggist was trying to keep her from having the medication she needed. The police studied the situation and tried to calm her. To the credit of the Rowayton police force, they managed to reduce her anger to a manageable sense of pique. They also told her that the druggist was well within his rights in refusing to refill the prescription.

Finally, she left the drugstore, and the situation was terminated.

At Thomas School's graduation ceremonies in 1974, Jean Harris was escorted by none other than Dr. Herman Tarnower.

* * * *

Although the exact date of her first meeting with Tarnower is not known, nor are the time and circumstances of her first date with him, it has become an established fact that the two of them started going out together as early as 1966, when Jean Harris first moved to Philadelphia.

Whether or not their companionship had romantic overtones from the beginning—or ever really did, for that matter—is not known. However, they did certainly become companions at social events from 1966, and were seen time and time again by their friends in the company of one another.

When Jean Harris moved to Connecticut to work at Thomas School, she found herself in close proximity to Hi Tarnower. Quite possibly that fact had something to do with her application for the job. Even if it did not, she certainly saw more of him once she had moved from Pennsylvania to Connecticut.

The two seemed ideally suited to one another, according to most people who knew them and saw them together, and it was noted that each admired the other for many reasons.

Tarnower liked beautiful women who had brains and good breeding. Jean Harris was certainly attractive and she was bright—almost brilliant—with an excellent blueblood background. It was obvious that Tarnower liked to be seen with her; it gave him a kind of prestige to be seen out with a well-turned-out, intelligent, and comely companion.

Jean Harris had no patience with stupidity. She had no patience with lack of taste. And she had no patience with any sign of the qualities of a loser in a man. Tarnower was charismatic, energetic, brainy, and a man with a sense of style.

"He was a 'gentlemen's gentleman,' extremely well-liked and respected," said one acquaintance. "A man with class, who walked with a regal air."

He had all the social nuances that brought him attention from the people he met. Jean Harris instinctively understood this from the moment she met him. And he had the proper instincts that guided him like radar toward the right people.

"He numbered among his friends the cream of society," a Purchase neighbor said of him.

On Tarnower's part, he respected Jean Harris for her ability to carry herself regally, the way a woman, in Tarnower's mind, should carry herself. What if she was a bit overbearing sometimes? What if she did tend to overstep her bounds in society? She knew how to carry it off.

Mostly, he respected her brains and her conversational abilities. She was someone he could talk to, not about medicine, or about the small everyday things that amuse most people, but about lofty subjects that most people might think were esoteric and arcane.

On Jean Harris's part, she understood one thing about Hi Tarnower that many other people did not understand. Tarnower tended to be a martinet, almost, in attitude sometimes. He wanted things done right. He needed military discipline in people surrounding him—particularly when he was at work.

Jean Harris had come from a family in which the head—her father—was in the military service. Part of her own authoritarian bearing was directly inherited from him. She knew exactly how Tarnower felt about doing the "right thing" at the "right time." He was in the top rank of human beings, and Jean Harris respected him for it, knowing that she herself was in the top rank too.

They seemed to embellish one another. At least, that is the way it looked to their friends who saw them with increasing frequency over the years at social events around Westchester County and New York.

Jean Harris's finishing school background—even though she had in truth never been to one!—resonated with Hi Tarnower's Ivy League/Establishment patina—although he was by no means an Establishment person!

Their relationship was excellent. People who knew them together understood that they were companions. They were seen everywhere. They were invited to the best places, and in turn invited the best people to Tarnower's place.

Jean Harris had been searching around the area for a house, and finally found one in Mahopac, New York. The name of the town is pronounced <u>Mah-Hope-Ic</u>, incidentally, not <u>May-oh-Pac</u>. The house was only a 45-minute drive from Thomas School. Coincidentally, it was just about the same distance from the home of Hi Tarnower in Purchase, New York.

Ironically enough, in view of what happened later, her house was located in a secluded area of Mahopac just off Bullet Hole Road! (Shades of Agatha Christie and the Tragic Irony she loved so.) She signed the papers for the place in 1975, and apparently felt that everything in her life was coming to a fine and full autumnal glow.

Her sons were both adults and away, and she had no problems except that her relationship with Hi Tarnower was seemingly stalled at an impasse—the fact, of course, that Tarnower didn't want to marry, and she did. She could not, apparently, understand why he would not break his long-standing rule about marriage—and marry her!

It was the one shadow in her otherwise sunny life.

Then, quite suddenly, everything fell apart. The inevitable occurred. Sometime in 1975 Thomas School closed, unable to reverse its declining enrollment. It was caught in the same financial bind that had closed dozens of other private girls' schools of the same kind—a financial problem that had become a national trend during the 1970s.

Jean Harris found herself quite abruptly and quite painfully out of a job. Her sons were both grown up and no burden to her now, but she did like to enjoy life and needed money to carry out her own plans.

Finally she took a job as a sales administration manager for a firm located in New York City. The company, Allied Maintenance Corporation, supplies janitors for buildings like Madison Square Garden and other large facilities in the big city. She was paid $32,500 a year for the job.

But for a woman who had the high ideals of a girls' school headmistress, the job was more a chore than a position. There was little glamour in the work. In fact, it must have seemed to be a bit grubby. Soon she tired of her responsibilities, and apparently wearied of her environment as well.

New York was not the nicest place in the world to work, either. But first and foremost, she did miss the familiar environment of private education, where she was dealing with people with backgrounds similar to her own.

To Allied's director of personnel, Jean Harris

seemed nothing out of the ordinary. She was a "normal individual as far as I know."

But she kept casting around for work that would take her out of the city and into those more familiar surroundings of academia. Finally, in 1977 she applied for the position of headmistress at a private girls' school in Greenway, Virginia, a village near McLean in Fairfax County—just over the Potomac River from Washington, D.C.

4

The Headmistress (II)

Founded in 1906 by Lucy Madeira, the private girls' high school in Fairfax County, Virginia, was called after its founder quite simply Madeira School.

Located in the midst of a 381-acre campus about twelve miles from downtown Washington, the school itself was nestled on a bluff overlooking the Potomac River.

Most of its buildings were set so far back in the rolling countryside that no one could see them from the Georgetown Pike, which wandered along through the terrain nearby, parallel to the Potomac.

Outside the white fence that surrounded the school there was no sign to identify the property of the Madeira School.

Tuition cost about $7,000 for boarding students, and about $4,200 a year for day students. In spite of the high cost, everyone around the area wanted to attend Madeira. Every year the admission office rejected about four applicants for every one it accepted.

The school had been located first in a row house near Dupont Circle in downtown Washington. When it moved to its present campus in 1931, the image of Madeira was permanently established. Physically, its buildings were built in a traditional Georgian-type architectural style, two stories high and facing in on a large center quadrangle of grass and trees.

Near the main gate of the campus a large stable and an indoor ring for riding horses had been built. The official opinion of school officials was that it was one of the largest indoor riding rings in the East.

The campus was thus a picture-book study of tree-shaded walkways, beautiful Georgian brick buildings, some of which contained drawing rooms with Chippendale furniture, and a magnificent view of the Potomac River rushing below.

There was a library with 20,000 books, a modernistic science building that had won a series of architectural awards, and a full-time faculty of 32, plus nine part-timers. Its students were enrolled in grades 9 through 12, exactly as in most traditional four-year high schools throughout the country.

With its high tuition and the famed riding ring near its front gate, Madeira was recognized by those in the know as a "horsey sort of social school." But it wasn't *really* a true horsey school at all.

"The horses are there, but most of the girls don't ride them now," a student once said. "It's a sort of passé thing now, you know."

About two out of three of the students were boarders, living in the very comfortable double rooms that lined the interior hallways of the brick and casement-windowed brick structures. Although the girls shared their quarters two to a room, they hardly lived in any kind of royal splendor.

"Not only do students clean their own rooms, but they rake leaves on the school grounds," one of the officials said recently, "and serve meals to each other at dinner."

More than 60 percent of the students came from Virginia, Maryland, and the District of Columbia.

Among the alumnae of Madeira were such luminaries of the Washington scene as Katherine Graham, chairman of the Washington Post Company, and Ann Swift, a U.S. foreign service officer now being held hostage in Iran.

The school now had twelve black students and were seeking more; up into the 1960s there were no blacks at Madeira. About one Madeira student in ten received financial aid.

The academic grind for the students was tough. It involved study hours from 8 a.m. to 3:30 p.m. four days a week, after which they became involved in compulsory extracurricular activities until 4:30 p.m. Most classes had about ten to twelve students. There was a heavy dose of mathematics at Madeira—a rare thing for a girls' school today.

Wednesday was an off-day for sophomores, juniors, and seniors—off from the campus, that is—when they worked as unpaid interns in congressional offices, nonprofit organizations, and museums, or as volunteers in hospitals, day-care centers, schools and nursing homes.

The *Insider's Guide to Prep Schools*, published in 1979 by the Yale Daily News, wrote, tongue in cheek:

"Madeira offers very adequate preparation if you are interested in marrying a nineteenth century English Lord." Then it added, to ameliorate the wound: "The school also tries to prepare its students for life in twentieth-century America . . . You can get a good education here . . . . Most Madeira students love their school, and it's easy to see why."

Current students included the daughters of Senator Malcom Wallop, Republican of Wyoming, ABC television reporter Sam Donaldson and commentator Eric Severeid, as well as the granddaughter of the late former vice-president Nelson Rockefeller. Today the school has an enrollment of 324 students.

When she learned what Madeira was and walked around the campus, Jean Harris knew that this was indeed a place she would be able to call her home. She crossed her fingers mentally, put her best foot forward, and prepared to appear before the search committee of the school administration.

She was one of about 80 applicants for the job.

The committee saw the most qualified of the applicants, and thinned down the ranks to a manageable roomful. These the committee interviewed, not once but several times.

There was no secret that Madeira, like most academic institutions of secondary school learning, had been having trouble keeping up with the changing lifestyle that had infected most of the young women of the country in the 1960s.

Even in the 1970s, permissivism and the laid-back attitude of the 1960s was still pervasive on the academic scene. But times were changing, and that permissivism which had been an accepted thing had now become a target for the administrators of many schools, especially private ones.

Discipline and integrity—those were the keys to the future of schools like Madeira, or they really had nowhere to go at all. As a matter of fact, those words reflected clearly the attitudes and opinions of the founder of Madeira school—Lucy Madeira.

"Keep calm at the very center of your being," had been one of her most quoted sayings.

"Function in disaster," she had said. "Finish in style."

As for the disruptive and radical changes that had occurred in the campus atmosphere of the 1960s, Madeira School motto had something to say for that, too.

"*Festinate lente.*"

Any noble Roman would recognize the saying: "Make haste slowly." In other words, change can be for the better, but it is best not to make change simply for the sake of change.

The rather unstable quality of the lifestyle of the late 1970s had prompted the search committee at Madeira to try to locate someone who had capabilities well above the average—particularly the capability of tightening up academic requirements at the school, and at the same time instilling a sense of real discipline.

A martinet was certainly not needed, but someone who understood discipline, law and order, and had a concept of conviction and integrity. Although security was not a problem at Madeira, there had been one most upsetting incident which had occurred in 1973.

It was, in effect, a blot on the escutcheon of Madeira, which up to that time had always

66

boasted of a spotless past. It was in that year that a well-publicized murder had occurred on the grounds of the exclusive and isolated campus.

The victim was a young girl fourteen years of age who was discovered dead just behind the Madeira School chapel. Her body was partly nude, and had been tied to a tree. Fairfax County authorities, who had investigated the crime, said it was "one of the more brutal cases we've ever seen."

Although there were no specific facts to indicate exactly how the girl had died, she had apparently been beaten repeatedly, and, according to the Fairfax Commonwealth District Attorney, Robert Horan, there was some indication of sexual assault.

Her identity was never revealed outside the confines of the school and her immediate family because of critical illness of two members of her family. Just before her body was found, a fourteen-year-old student at Madeira had been reported missing. The discovery of the body ended the search.

No one was ever caught or punished for the killing. The crime was never solved. The story caused tremors throughout the entire community—particularly among the well-to-do parents of the students at the school.

Madeira authorities felt the school must somehow tighten up its security and its discipline to a degree that the murder could not be in any way laid to the manner in which the school functioned.

One way to do this was to acquire a headmistress whose probity and sense of discipline would be beyond reproach. And that was the reason the search committee was looking for a person slightly different from the ordinary headmistress.

Was Jean Harris the person who could steer a clear course for Madeira in the years to come —in view of the permissivism established in the 1960s and in view of the savage crime that had occurred on the grounds of Madeira? Could she bring back discipline and a sense of decorum to students who had spent their formative years in the storm-tossed vessel of permissivism, doing their own thing, obeying only the dictates of their own slipshod morality?

Jean Harris thought she was the right person. She told the committee so.

Most of the members of the committee agreed with her. But they wanted reassurances of their own judgments. Certain members of the search committee were delegated to make attempts to check into Jean Harris's record at Thomas School in Connecticut.

Extensive investigation was difficult because the Connecticut school had closed its doors and its faculty members were scattered to the four winds, making it almost impossible to locate them for recommendations.

Nevertheless, several of them were found, and from them, Jean Harris received very strong support. At least, so said one of the vice presidents at Madeira School. After some discussion, it was decided to tender her an offer of the position. She would be getting an amount somewhere in the neighborhood of $20,000 a year.

Jean Harris knew that would mean having to

take a salary cut of nearly $10,000 a year, but after some soul-searching, she knew she would be better off in Virginia as far from the rugged Manhattan rat race as she could get. She knew she would be happy to trade the daily hassle with the train, the traffic, the noise, and the intense competition of the city with the peace and quiet of the rolling woodlands and the hightoned atmosphere of academia.

She handed in her notice at Allied. She had worked there for a year and a half. Within weeks she was packed up and ready to move to Fairfax County, Virginia. Her residence as headmistress of Madeira would be in an elegant red-brick house called "The Hill."

In July, 1977, Jean Harris moved and settled into the life at Madeira without a hitch. She felt more at home there than she had at the job in New York. And, she could drive to her Mahopac house in Putnam County, New York on the weekends and holidays within hours. She would then be only a short distance from Hi Tarnower's house in Purchase.

From the beginning of her years at Madeira, Jean Harris was liked and respected for her outlook and character. One of the parents who met her described her as an "enlightened individual." According to another, she settled down to become one of the best headmistresses in the history of the school.

However, there were differing opinions of her stewardship at Madeira. To those she punished, she was known as a tough disciplinarian. Some called her "too critical and overbearing!" Those who escaped censure, called her a good headmistress.

Parents were apt to think of her as someone who did a great deal to improve the quality of education at the school and to increase school spirit. She kept herself available as headmistress, with the door to her residence at "The Hill" on the campus always open so that students could come in and chat with her during weekends when she was on campus.

It was not long after she had come to Madeira that the image of Jean Harris on campus came into focus, and she was known mostly for her talks about "integrity" in personal and business life. She gave frequent talks at assemblies about the need for control and decency.

"She has said the word 'integrity' so many times that some of the students call her Integrity Harris," one student said.

After her arrival, she stiffened the school's honor code, and lectured the girls frequently about their responsibility not to cheat or violate school rules involving the use of drugs.

Nevertheless, it was emphasized that she was not considered an inflexible disciplinarian. She would speak at assembly each Monday morning about current events, public responsibility, and she would lead them, with her loud, clear voice, in singing hymns.

She became popular among many of the students. She was given a standing ovation from mothers attending a school function one year when she said many of the students at Madeira needed strict discipline. At that time she announced that she had made the Georgetown area of Washington off-limits to students from the school.

An educational consulting firm studying her

work gave her high marks in 1979 as an administrator, calling her work "properly organized, responsible, and effective. . . . We are impressed with what the headmistress has accomplished in her two years at the school . . . ."

And in spite of being a stickler for discipline, she was liked by the students well enough so that when her dog ran away, she was given a new one named Cider as a Halloween gift.

Little was known at Madeira about Jean Harris's private life. Indeed, it was not suspected that she had any private life, other than her professional existence as the headmistress of Madeira School.

No one knew whom she saw when she traveled to Mahopac in New York on weekends. No one even thought to ask. When she went away on trips during the vacation months, no one pried into her private life. She revealed little about her personal affairs to anyone on the campus.

It was as if the real Jean Harris existed somewhere outside the environs of Madeira School. And, in fact, who was the real Jean Harris? Wasn't she the detached, cool, impersonal, and integrity-oriented person the students at Madeira knew? Was she ever a fiery, irrational, hot-headed, and profane woman who only assumed a mask of calm and placidity?

Wasn't she really the *proper* woman who taught the daughters of the prominent Washington personalities how to be reserved, well-bred, and correct? Could she really effectively hide a cruel cutting edge to her personality?

In appearance, Harris was always slender, attractive, intelligent and witty, equally at home in an English saddle and at a Washington cocktail party, someone who seemed always to be in control of herself and her surroundings.

And what about her relationship with Tarnower? No one—at least on the surface—knew about it at Madeira. They had met in 1966, had often appeared together at social gatherings, and had made no secret of their friendship. Were they merely close friends? Were they passionate lovers? What was the real relationship between the headmistress and the cardiologist?

The real Jean Harris obviously existed—but far from the boundaries of Madeira. Her inner drives and ambitions were obviously at odds with her outward appearance of smooth and silken calm.

But that would all change one day. Those at Madeira who knew nothing about her relationship with Tarnower would soon learn of it. It was the Scarsdale Diet that made Tarnover's name a household word and catapulted him into national fame, but his connection with Jean Harris would soon make him even more famous after his scandalous death.

5

The Diet

Cardiology was a newly introduced, slowly developing branch of science when Hi Tarnower first decided to concentrate on its study. But by the time World War II was over and the postwar era of prosperity and affluence had settled in throughout America, cardiology as a subbranch of science and as a medical specialty had begun to attain a stature and popularity that no one would have predicted in its early days.

Tarnower now found himself anchored to a rising star. He could do no wrong. Deaths from heart conditions and ailments associated with the heart outnumbered deaths from all other ailments—including cancer. Cardiology, which had started out as a study of the heart itself and the treatment of heart conditions, now inexorably was becoming a type of preventive medicine by means of which the patient was advised on how to keep his heart from developing diseases of all kinds.

The culprit found in most cases of heart disease was soon isolated as avoirdupois—too much fat. Of all the nations on earth, Americans in the Twentieth Century ate more than anyone else. They would be stupid not to overeat—America had devised the best production of food, it had developed the best distribution of foodstuffs, it had invented the best systems of preparation of food in advance of serving.

Excessive eating led to one thing in particular: too much body fat. The country's very success in producing food and marketing edibles was becoming its downfall, causing the deaths of millions of people because of their affluence and superabundant food intake.

To curtail so much death from overeating, it was necessary to reduce the poundage on the average American human frame. And in order to cut down on those pounds caused by overweight—the condition that inevitably caused a great deal of additional stress to put on the action of the heart—doctors, cardiologists, in particular, advised their patients on the ways and means of reducing excess poundage.

The modus operandi of avoiding extra weight was so obvious that almost everyone tended to overlook it; it was simply not to eat so much food. But for people who had survived deprivation of one kind or another during the grim years of the Great Depression and the lean years of World War II—including the men who were away doing the fighting and the ones who were staying home rationing their food for the troops—it was difficult to cut down. The pleasure of eating as much as one wanted had become one of the reasons for fighting the war in the first place; it had become a fetish with the majority of the people in the country.

As philosophers have known for centuries, the human animal is not a logical animal. What seemed so obviously logical for the scientist was in no way the human animal's way. No one cared to give up even one bit of the food that was his now for the eating after so many years of "starvation."

The proverb says that there is no way one can have his cake and eat it too. By the same token, there is no way for one to eat and not eat, too. But in the post-war world, it soon became fashionable to pay little attention to what one was eating—but to pay great attention to one's proper weight. The way to weigh the proper amount, no matter how much one ate, was to indulge in food as much as one wanted, and then counter-indulge in its cure—diet.

In those post-war years, diet soon became the "in" thing to do. The person who wasn't on a diet was simply not "with it." There was nothing new about diets, of course. Diets were as old as mankind.

Every bit of food the body eats supplies energy to the body. In fact, that food is "burned" by the body in the production of energy. The amount of food eaten corresponds to the amount of food "burned." If more food is taken in than is burned to produce energy, the body stores up the accumulated food as fat, to be ready for burning at a later time to produce energy necessary for its actions.

It becomes obvious that the body which consumes only as much food as is needed to produce energy to see the body through its daily motions does not accumulate fat.

Science has long known how to measure the amount of heat produced. Units of heat production were calibrated by Joseph Black in 1760. His machine to measure these energy units was called a calorimeter.

Even before that time, the French physicist Antoine Lavoisier had formulated the law of thermodynamics which stated that heat energy could not be created from nothing. In other words, the number of calories produced by burning would exactly equal the number of calories supplied. Calories not used by burning would be stored up.

It was obvious that by limiting the number of calories supplied to the body to the number of calories it would burn, the body would not be able to store up added calories in fat. Thus, from the beginning, modern dietetic laws were essentially linked with the counting of calories.

Actually, the calorie referred to in modern diets is not the calorie referred to in scientific studies. That diet calorie familiar to anyone counting the calories in foods is actually 1000 times the scientific calorie—a kilo calorie. A food calorie produces 1000 times the amount of heat represented by a small calorie.

It was discovered that if the eater cuts down the number of calories he eats by 500 a day, he will lose a pound a week. If he cuts down on 1000 calories a day, he will lose two pounds in a week. This very rough equation assumes that the eater won't change his physical activities at all. Lots of exercise will burn more calories; no exercise will burn less calories—hence, more fat.

A rule of thumb used by the American Medical Association says that the person leading a moderately active life burns about 15 calories every day per pound. For example, the male weighing 150 pounds should take in 2250 calories a day to maintain that weight. More caloric intake than that will lead to a gain in weight; significantly fewer calories will cause a loss in weight.

However, it is dangerous to go below 1000-1200 calories a day, unless the dieter is under a doctor's supervision. With so little food, the body does not get enough minerals or other necessary nutrients.

For a very sedentary dieter, the number 15 should be reduced to 12—12 calories per pound per day.

Of course, there were always all kinds of diets devised in order to keep the public's weight at the proper minimum. By using the 1000-1200 calories a day as a parameter within which to keep the average person's intake, all varieties of menus can be arranged. But the breakdown is complicated. Intake must be broken down into the various types of food needed for the healthy body: protein, fat, and carbohydrates—including starch and sugar.

One of the most influential guidelines for a diet has been made by the U.S. Senate's Select Committee on Nutrition and Human Needs. "Dietary Goals for the U.S.," the paper the committee produced, is not really a diet at all, but a consolidation of the findings of the best nutritional research to date.

"Obesity," states the report, "resulting from the over-consumption of calories is a major risk factor in killer disease. Therefore, it is extremely important either to maintain an optimal weight or to alter one's weight to reach an optimal level. Obesity is associated with the onset and clinical progression of diseases such as hypertension, diabetes mellitus, heart disease, and gall bladder disease. It may also modify the quality of one's life."

The committee recommends six dietary goals:

1. Increase the consumption of carbohydrates (starches) and "naturally occurring sugars" (in fruits) from 28 percent of daily total calories to 58 percent.

2. Reduce the amount of refined sugar from 18 percent to 10 percent.

3. Reduce consumption of fat from 40 percent to 30 percent.

4. Balance the kinds of fats so that 10 percent of daily calories are saturated fats (such as butter) and another 10 percent polyunsaturated fats (such as safflower and corn oil).

5. Hold daily cholesterol consumption to 300 milligrams a day (slightly less than the amount in one egg yolk).

6. Eat no more than 5 grams of table salt a day.

Those recommendations translate into calories from carbohydrates, fat, and protein as follows:

● About 58 percent of the caloric intake should be carbohydrates, including both starches and sugars.

● No more than 30 percent of the total calories should be polyunsaturated or animal source fat, which includes butterfat.

● Only 12 percent of calories should come from protein sources—meat, milk, fish, chicken, eggs, grains, beans, and vegetables.

The U.S. Senate Diet is presented to give an idea of one type of diet that is suggested for the average person. As can be noted, it is high in carbohydrates and low in protein. There are other diets which are high in protein and low in carbohydrates.

The high-protein diet has been around more than a hundred years. Fat takes a longer time to digest than protein and carbohydrates. Because it is slower in digestion, it affords a more prolonged feeling of satiety than the other major nutrients. Fats fight hunger. Proteins and carbohydrates are quickly consumed. A high fat diet is a diet that causes little suffering.

The most famous one, which produced a best-seller back in London in 1864, was devised for a man named William Banting whose chief claim to fame was that he had manufactured the coffin in which the Duke of Wellington was buried. A corpulent, affluent man, Banting had developed a bad earache for which he went to William Harvey, a famous ear surgeon of the day.

Harvey had just returned from Paris, where he had been listening to lectures of Claude Bernard, a physiologist who had been discussing the evils of sugars and the relationship of diabetes mellitus to the intake of sugar. It was Bernard's theory that diabetes could be controlled by avoiding sugar.

By the time Harvey saw the 60-year-old Banting, he decided that Banting was suffering from a pain induced by excess fat. Harvey theorized that the excess fat pressing on the eustachian tube—a narrow tunnel connecting the middle ear to the back of the throat—was causing Banting's pain. His procedure was to cause Banting to lose weight so that fat would be dissipated, and the pain lessened.

Impressed by Bernard's discussions of sugar and its relationship to excess weight, Harvey devised a unique diet for Banting: meat, mutton, bacon, and fish—with bare minimum of sugar, bread, beer, and potatoes.

Banting adhered to the diet, and to his amazement, lost the excess weight he had always had, going from 202 pounds to 156 pounds in a year. Also, the pain in his inner ear went away. He was so happy with the high-fat reducing diet he had been using that he composed a pamphlet called *Letter on Corpulence* and published it in London. It was an almost instant success, becoming a best-seller immediately.

Thousands of Britishers read the pamphlet, and followed the diet. It was a fad, like many diets, and within a few years interest in it had died out. Nevertheless, it was revived in the late 1800s by physicians attending the Earl of Salisbury. To get the fat old Earl's weight and girth down, they prescribed a diet of meat. The Earl and his menu are still with us in a name we see on many a restaurant menu—Salisbury Steak. Salisbury Steak, as any fast-food eater knows, is simply ground beef, also known as hamburger.

In the beginning of this century, weight-reducing diets began to concentrate on counting calories and limiting foods within a balanced diet. But by the middle of the century Alfred W. Pennington, M.D., head of the medical division of E.I. Dupont de Namours and Co. formulated a diet for the Dupont employees which would enable them to eat fat and get thin.

To eat fat and get thin, the dieter must restrict his intake of carbohydrates. Experiments at the Russell Sage Institute in 1928 had indicated that a dieter's meal could consist of two to three ounces of fat and six to nine ounces of meat—in other words, fat meat. Pennington decided to restrict the carbohydrates and increase the fat. His diet became known as the Dupont Diet. It was all the rage in the 1950s.

At about the time Herman Tarnower opened his Scarsdale Medical Center with his four partners, he had been experimenting with a diet to give his overweight patients. He knew all about the high-fat low-carbohydrate diets and knew they were successful, but he did not like the amount of fat consumed in the diets. Instead of increasing the amount of fat at the expense of carbohydrates, he decided to switch around and increase the protein rather than the fat at the expense of carbohydrates.

He suspected that carbohydrates were the real villian in the diets people struggled to maintain—mainly because they were quick to be assimilated, leaving the dieter always hungry. Proteins, too were digested swiftly, but not so swiftly as carbohydrates.

Mainly, Tarnower was fascinated with the possibilities of the high protein diet because it would enable him to allow his patients what they loved best—meat, poultry, fish, and eggs—and, this was the key to the success of the diet, "plenty of it."

"I never sat down to create a great diet," Tarnower once said. "It just became one."

He never made any bones about inventing a new diet. He admitted that he simply put together ideas from many other high-protein, low-fat, low-carbohydrate, low-calorie diets that had been around for years. These diets had been tried many times before. He simply perfected his own variation.

Of course buying lean meats was a deadly blow to the budget, but in Scarsdale, budgets didn't matter too much. Everyone had money. By eating good lean meats, a dieter could consume almost as much as he wanted—within limits. But carbohydrates were definitely a no-no.

He devised his formula so that the diet was a combination of 43 percent protein, 22.5 percent fat, and 34.5 percent carbohydrate that would provide 1000 calories a day.

(It is interesting to compare his formula with that suggested by the U.S. Senate Select Committee on Nutrition and Human Needs: 12 percent protein, 30 percent fat, and 58 percent carbohydrates).

"If a dieter overeats, he or she can get up to 1,400, 1,500, or 1,600 calories," Tarnower said in an article about the diet.

The average weight loss would be about a pound a day, according to his calculation. Since the diet was severe in its restriction of carbohydrates, Tarnower never intended anyone to go on the diet longer than two weeks.

"My diet is simple and safe," he said. "People are willing to put up with the discipline and deprivation necessary because they know it works."

The Scarsdale Diet was simplicity itself. Basically, it consisted of a strict accounting of every dish in every meal for two weeks. There were no restrictions on the quantity of foods allowed on the diet: proteins like roast chicken and pot cheese could be eaten in quantity, for instance.

Discipline otherwise was strict: the dieter was required to follow, for the full two weeks, a day-by-day menu that allowed absolutely no substitution.

First of all, however, there were important rules.

● A heart patient could not take on the diet.

● No substitutes or deviations from the diet were allowed.

● No alcoholic beverages.

● No eating between meals, except raw celery and carrots.

● No skin or visible fat was allowed on the meat eaten.

● No butter, margarine, or sauce allowed on vegetables.

● No oil or mayonnaise on the salads, only lemon or vinegar.

● The dieter could eat only foods stated in the menu.

● No overloading of the stomach allowed.

The diet itself was the same for two weeks.

Breakfast was the same each day:

● Grapefruit, or fruit in season

● Toasted slice of dry protein bread

● Black coffee or tea

Lunch was different each day:

● Monday: cold cuts of lean meat; tomatoes, coffee, tea, or diet soda

● Tuesday: fruit salad, any kind, unlimited quantity; coffee, tea, or diet soda

● Wednesday: tuna fish or salmon salad with lemon or vinegar dressing; grapefruit or other fresh fruit; coffee, tea, or diet soda

● Thursday: two eggs, low-fat cottage cheese; zucchini, string beans or stewed tomatoes; 1 slice dry protein toast, coffee, tea, or diet soda

● Friday: assorted cheese slices; spinach; 1 slice dry protein toast; coffee, tea, or diet soda

● Saturday: fruit salad (any kind, unlimited quantity); coffee, tea, or diet soda

● Sunday: chicken or turkey; tomatoes, carrots; cabbage, broccoli, or cauliflower; grapefruit or other fresh fruit; coffee, tea, or diet soda

Dinner was different each day:

● Monday: fish; combination salad (unlimited quanity); 1 slice dry protein toast; grapefruit or other fresh fruit; coffee, tea, or diet soda

● Tuesday: plenty of steak or broiled, lean hamburger; tomatoes; lettuce, celery, olives; brussel sprouts or cucumbers; coffee, tea, or diet soda

● Wednesday: roast lamb slices; celery, cucumbers, tomatoes; coffee, tea, or diet soda

● Thursday: chicken (roast, broiled, or barbecued); spinach, green peppers, string beans; coffee, tea, or diet soda

● Friday: fish; combination salad (unlimited fresh vegetables); 1 slice dry protein toast; coffee, tea, or diet soda

● Saturday: cold chicken or turkey; tomatoes and lettuce; grapefruit or other fresh fruit; coffee, tea, or diet soda

● Sunday: plenty of steak; tomatoes, celery, cucumbers or Brussel sprouts; coffee, tea, or diet soda

From the beginning, the diet *did* work, as Tarnower knew it would. There was, in fact, good scientific reasons why it worked—why it worked better than diets in the low-protein, high-carbohydrate diet category.

Scientists had already discovered that such a low-carbohydrate diet actually acted as a diuretic; that is, the consumption of the foods allowed acted to drive the water out of the body. Because the loss of water cuts down on the dieter's weight—a pint of water weighs about one pound, as any grammar school student knows—the diet began to work on the dieter almost immediately. All that was leaving the body during the first few days was water, *not* fat. And the water disappeared at a phenomenal rate—20 pounds in two weeks!

The rapid weight loss with Tarnower's diet was very appealing to the dieter. By the end of the two weeks, many dieters had lost up to 20 pounds. Since the diet lasted only fourteen days, the dieter was able then to eat anything he wanted to after that.

That was the point at which there could be discouragement.

The truth was, almost as quickly as the fluid was lost, it could return, and with a vengeance. The intake of only a moderate amount of carbohydrates and any fluid would simply stay in the body. And that intake would cause the lost weight to return—at the rate of a pound to each pint of fluid intake!

There was one other problem that the diet could cause. It was a problem associated with any restricted carbohydrate intake. There was a change in bodily metabolism. Below a certain daily intake in the number of grams of carbohydrate—nutritionists usually agree that the standard number is 60, but the actual number can vary widely with individuals—the body was forced to obtain energy mainly from fat it had stored up rather than from the usual carbohydrate supply used to provide quick energy.

This caused the body to enter a state known as ketosis. In other words, body fat was being burned at an accelerated rate. As a result, ketone bodies were building up in the blood. These were then excreted by the kidneys, along with valuable vitamins and minerals which then were used to help nourish the body.

Ketone bodies were discovered by scientists to curb the appetite. Some individuals in ketosis, they found, experienced an unpleasant taste sensation and sometimes varying degrees of nausea, all of which led to loss of appetite.

The state of ketosis was not particularly dangerous for a week or two weeks, which made the Scarsdale Diet safe. Nevertheless, ketosis did put a considerable strain on the kidneys. For that reason, pregnant women should never go into ketosis. Scientists also found evidence that ketosis caused excessive retention of uric acid. Excessive uric acid is associated with gout.

It was obvious that anyone who was going to be on a low-carbohydrate diet for more than two weeks, should have his uric acid and cholesterol levels tested regularly.

Nevertheless, for the average person not involved in any of the problems of health mentioned, the Scarsdale Diet as developed by Tarnower was fun to follow, it worked with rapid results, and it wasn't any kind of a hardship for a person with gourmet tastes.

It was the Scarsdale Diet's success with the affluent and the prominent that started its unprecedented popularity. Tarnower had a good practice, but he did not have thousands of patients. He simply had the number a good cardiologist would have.

These patients immediately told friends about the success of the diet. Tarnower made it a practice to give his diet to everyone who wanted it—patient or non-patient. When strangers wrote to his office, he would slip a mimeographed sheet describing the diet into an envelope and send it to them.

He did not believe in making money on something that was for the good of people, whether his patients or not. Because it was a diet that *worked*, people in all walks of life began using the Scarsdale Diet.

Show-business people—who needed to control their weight for public appearances—fell in love with the diet immediately. Soon even the gourmet restaurants in Hollywood were inserting notes on their menus attributing certain dishes to the Scarsdale Diet.

Its fame spread everywhere.

The media began picking up hints of it, and wrote about it. People from all over the world began sending in to Tarnower for a copy of the diet.

"I am told," he wrote, "that no diet has ever been so spontaneously and unaminously acclaimed as this one. At first it took off arithmetically—one patient telling another person. As word of mouth increased, its popularity grew geometrically, nationally and internationally."

In physical fitness classes everywhere teachers would distribute the Scarsdale Diet to their students, and recommended exercise to take off inches and firm up flesh while the Diet took off the pounds.

The Beach Point Club in Mamaroneck, New York, near Scarsdale, posted a notice on its bulletin boards and dining tables:

"The Scarsdale Diet. If you're on it, Beach Point has it. If you're not on it, you will be. Every lunch in the Pavilion, every regular dinner in the dining room has a Scarsdale Diet dish on the menu."

Tarnower reported that a woman who was on jury duty took along a Scarsdale Medical Diet lunch box with her to the jury room and noticed with some surprise that others in the courtroom had the same diet.

A writer from the *New York Times Magazine* named Alexandra Penney got interested in the diet and while writing a column on beauty that was a feature in the weekly section described the diet in an article titled "Shape-Up Time."

"A vice president of Bloomingdale's was shown the printed diet by the owner of a fish restaurant," she said, "decided to try it, lost 20 pounds in 14 days and claims he was never hungry and never tired."

Westchester Magazine picked up the diet and ran a short item about it. "A Diet People Are Talking About . . . 'as much as a twenty pound loss in two weeks is not unusual' . . . those who have tried it insist it's the only one that works."

Family Circle magazine wrote, "Here's a diet that took the town of Scarsdale, N.Y. by storm, and now may well be sweeping the country. With it you lose up to 20 pounds in 14 days—without ever going hungry.

"This is the no-hunger, no-hassle diet that the in-the-know big losers have been passing on to their friends coast-to-coast. It's the *easiest diet ever*. In exactly eight days, I had lost exactly eight pounds!

"It's an enormous relief not to have to count calories or weigh food or worry about quantities . . . you lose weight without a lot of fuss."

New York Times writer Georgia Dullea wrote an article on the diet, under the headline: "If It's Friday, It Must Be Spinach and Cheese." She wrote: "The Scarsdale Diet: This is where the losers live, the real losers. This is the home of the famous 14-day Scarsdale Diet. . . . Weight losses of up to 20 pounds in two weeks are reported here. Rarely do dieters feel hungry or cranky. . . The Scarsdale diet is spreading. . . . Requests are coming from as far away as California and Mexico. Now London is ringing up about the Scarsdale diet. . . . Everywhere you go people are talking about this diet. . . ."

In *Sunday Woman*, a one-time newspaper supplement magazine, Anthony Dias Blue called the diet "THE ULTIMATE DIET. . . so named by a friend who has been on every diet ever invented . . . she looked relaxed, slim, crowed, 'I've been on Dr. Tarnower's Scarsdale Medical Diet, AND IT WORKS! I lost 18 pounds in 14 days, and I'm able to KEEP IT OFF!'

"The diet is tasty and filling; you can order it in any restaurant and follow it easily at home.

". . . Why the popularity of the diet? BECAUSE IT WORKS!"

Hundreds of dieters wrote in their appreciation to Tarnower.

One of his own patients wrote: "It's three

years now since I went on your diet and slimmed down from 152 pounds to my desired 118 pounds. I've kept trim on your simple Two-On-Two-Off program without any trouble. As for my health, as you know from my regular checkups, most of my medical problems have disappeared. I feel better than ever. My husband keeps saying how wonderful it is to have a slim, attractive wife again, but he can hardly match my own delight about the 'new' me.''

And another: "I lost 14 pounds in the first two weeks on your diet and our grown son lost 20. That's 34 pounds in our family already. You are really and truly responsible for the shedding of a lot of unwanted pounds in this area. We're absolutely delighted with the results of the diet.''

And still another: "I didn't have more than 10 pounds to lose, which I lost quickly on your diet. Results were almost immediate. I found that the daily food combinations on your menu didn't leave me hungry in the least. Best of all, I had no craving for food at night—that's always been my biggest problem. I thank you for the time and energy put into something that works and is *fun*.''

And so on.

The cardiologist had suddenly become a diet genius. He was on his way to becoming a household name, although he didn't really know it at the time.

6

The Book

People in the publishing business know that books on dieting have not always been perennial best-sellers.

Back in 1864, William Banting's pamphlet titled *Letters on Corpulence* created a big stir throughout the English-speaking world. But from that year until 1922, when Lulu Hunt Peters published *Diet and Health with Key to the Calories,* there was a dearth of diet books even in the book stalls.

The Peters book shot up into the best-seller list in 1922, when it was Number Four on the Nonfiction List, with a sale of about 100,000. In 1923 it had sunk to Number Six, but was still considered a strong seller, with a total of about 200,000 sales—at that time a prodigious feat of salesmanship.

In 1924 the Peters book came on full force and was Number One! It was still Number One in 1925, and sank into third place in 1926, after which it vanished from sight.

From 1926 it was not until the 1960s and the 1970s that the publishing world could count once again on the strength of the diet book as a sales item. First came Herman Taller's *Calories Don't Count,* which appeared in 1961 and attained the Number Eight rank. After a slow start, it shot up into the Number One slot in 1962, with total sales at that time of 1,100,000—in hardback! At that time a million plus sale was a high figure for a hardback book.

Then came Irwin Maxwell Stillman's *The Doctor's Quick Weight Loss Diet,* Robert C. Atkin's *Dr. Atkins' Diet Revolution,* and Robert Linn's *The Last Chance Diet.*

Of those, Atkins' was one of the biggest sellers, racking up total sales of 5,250,000 in hardback and paperback.

Theodore Berland, a syndicated science-and-medicine writer who was an expert on the diet craze and who wrote columns about dieting, explained the phenomenon once by telling Ray Walters of the *New York Times,* "The 20's, the 60's and the 70's were narcissistic decades. Dieters are predominantly women, whose concern isn't their health, but a desire to appear 'sexy.' "

"Not so!" protested numerous Women's Libbers, pointing out that dieting was not necessarily for the purpose of becoming a sex object, but for the purpose of attaining good health.

The fact that some diet books have been huge successes does not mean that all diet books sell well. The trick is to get a diet book with the right gimmick; then it will sell "sensationally well," rather than just "very well."

Because of the various types of diet books on the market, it is sometimes difficult to come by a new and dramatic diet that looks exciting and also works well.

Diets, unfortunately, are faddish by nature. They come and go like styles in dress—short skirts one year, long skirts the next, big hats this year, no hats the next, and so on.

Certain diets that are the most successful are eventually killed off by their own extreme popularity. For example, Dr. Robert Atkins' diet book called *Dr. Atkins' Diet Revolution* had a phenomenal sales history with over five million sales over a period of several years after its publication in 1973. But after its sales dwindled, the diet it advanced was deader than the proverbial doornail—at least with the majority of American dieters.

That doesn't mean that the Atkins book was not controversial and had smooth sailing all the way once it was published. The exact opposite is true. It became one of the most controversial diet books of the time. Its very controversiality apparently helped stimulate sales.

The problem with the Atkins diet was that it was essentially the same kind of diet that had been promulgated in the Victorian Era by William Banting: a high-fat/low-carbohydrate (and low-protein) diet.

Soon after its publication, an American Medical Association panel issued a press release warning that the dietary recommendations in the Atkins book were "unscientific and potentially dangerous to the health." The AMA was particularly unhappy about the fact that the book recommended a diet that activated fat-mobilizing hormones. These in turn caused stored fat to be turned into carbohydrates. The AMA's concern was that the diet advocated unlimited intake of saturated fats and cholesterol-rich foods; at that time these foods were current villains which the AMA was assailing.

Atkins responded to the charge and denied that his diet was unscientific and that it was potentially dangerous to the health. Shortly after that, the Medical Society of the County of New York denounced the Atkins no-carbohydrate diet as "unscientific, unbalanced and potentially dangerous" to persons prone to kidney disease, heart disease, and gout.

A spokesman for the group stated that if the Atkins diet was followed by a pregnant woman, it could impair the intellectual development of her unborn child. The diet was designed in such a way that it would cause a state of ketosis.

Atkins retaliated with a statement that his findings were based on clinical observation of 10,000 obese subjects studied for a period of nine years.

Then, several days later, a man named Joseph Kottler cited Atkins in a $7.5 million damage suit, charging that the Atkins diet had led to a heart attack he had sustained as a result of Atkins's "medical negligence and malpractice."

Atkins, his associate Dr. I. Mason and the David McKay Company, publishers of the Atkins book, were named in the suit. The suit charged that the Atkins diet, which restricted intake of carbohydrates but was rich in fats and cholesterol, had led the litigant to angina pectoris and heart attack.

The attendant publicity apparently did not hurt the sale of the book a bit. The suit proved to be a nuisance suit and was apparently settled out of court. And the diet went rolling merrily along. Then, after several years, it more or less sank out of sight.

Atkins wrote more books, and published

them, but none did so well as *Revolution*. That Atkins book was published by the David McKay Company, New York. Atkins gave credit on the contents page to Fran Gare and Helen Monica for the recipes and the menus in the text. The copyright was held by Atkins and Ruth West Herwood. In publishing jargon, that meant that the book was ghosted by Herwood. Although it is not necessarily true, many books by eminent medical practitioners, scientists, and other types of public personalities such as film and television stars are usually ghosted by professional writers.

In 1975 the David McKay Company had a large turnover in top talent after being sold to a conglomerate. It was that year that Eleanor and Kenneth Rawson, who were the guiding lights at McKay, left and formed their own company. Shortly after that James Wade, who had been an editor at McKay during the Rawson regime, and prior to that had been an editor at McMillan, joined the Rawsons and became part of the company, which changed its name to Rawson, Wade.

At this time, Eleanor Rawson was trying to line up a good diet book to match the runaway success of the Atkins book she had shepherded through at McKay. She had been amused when she read Dr. Irwin Maxwell Stillman's second diet book called *Dr. Stillman's 14-Day Shape-Up Program,* published by Delacourt Press. In it, Stillman had taken a number of gloves-off punches at Atkins and his diet.

Stillman's previous book, *The Doctor's Quick Inches-Off Diet* had been published by Prentice-Hall and paperbacked by Dell. He was a professional in the diet line, and to her he looked like a good bet.

Stillman had not done the writing of those two books all by himself; a professional writer named Samm Sinclair Baker had done the actual work for Stillman.

Baker, incidentally, had started out as an advertising executive, got bored with the frenetic business, and started free-lancing fiction. After writing a number of mystery novels—one of them was about an ad executive who became a private eye to solve a crime in the agency—he switched to do-it-yourself books, producing a book on gardening for the weekend gardener that surprised even Baker by its success.

The Stillman-Baker collaboration had done very well in the bookstalls and in the paperback stands in reprint. Rawson, Wade decided they wanted another diet book to put on an upcoming schedule and since Stillman had died of a heart attack in 1975, they approached Stillman's collaborator.

Would he look around for a good diet for a book for Rawson, Wade?

It didn't take Baker long to find one. He lived in Mamaroneck and had heard a number of people talking about the Scarsdale Diet. He himself had not tried the diet at that time, but did later on, along with his wife, and they found it quite successful.

"I examined a number of diets," Baker said, "found the Scarsdale Diet, but when I wrote to the Scarsdale Medical Center, to another doctor, I got no reply."

Although the Scarsdale Diet was known around and about at that time, it was not yet the blockbuster diet it later became. Tarnower's name was not yet linked to it. No one on the outside really knew *who* had dreamed it up.

Baker's letter apparently died in limbo amidst a welter of unopened junk mail at the Center. Or perhaps Tarnower was simply not interested. Whatever, it was never answered.

Baker, described once in the *New York Times* as "America's leading self-help author," was not above the ability to help himself. He wrote another letter to the clinic. This time somebody apparently read his request, and it was handed over to Tarnower. In due time Tarnower responded with a note to Baker.

"We agreed on a collaboration," Baker said. That was in 1977.

Actually, putting together a book—a whole 50,000-60,000 word book that might sell for from $7 to $10 and that was based on a fourteen-day diet—was no picnic for Sam Baker. The diet itself involved possibly three pages of copy. What he did was to sit down with Tarnower and suggest the doctor dream up some "special" recipes to accompany the basic diet.

Tarnower also agreed to prepare four different versions of the basic Scarsdale Diet—the Gourmet Diet, the Money-Saver Diet, the Vegetarian Diet, and the International Diet—for, respectively, gourmets, people on limited budgets, vegetarians, and dieters with internationally-oriented palates.

Tarnower added a special Keep Trim Diet to be followed for the two weeks after the Scarsdale Diet was finished.

In addition to the four alternates and the special Keep Trim Diet, Baker added a long section of typical questions and answers about dieting and about the Scarsdale Diet in order to fill out the book. After that, he taped some of Tarnower's medical exhortations—the kind of Gung-Ho speeches used to give heart to patients who were trying to lose weight but were discouraged.

For example:

● *"Chew! Chew! Chew!* I can't overemphasize that. It's a big help in dieting not to rush your eating. And you'll enjoy every bite more."

● *"When you feel satisfied, STOP!* I can't stress enough that overloading your stomach is a health hazard, aside from piling on overweight. I read somewhere that obesity is the penalty for exceeding the *'feed limit.'* "

● *"Don't look back.* Some overweights maintain that since they've always failed on diets in the past, there's no hope for the future. Take this tip from Confucius: '*What is past*, one cannot amend. . . . For the future, one can *always provide.*' "

Baker worked with Tarnower day and night for more than four months. Their relationship was strictly business—the business of getting the book ready for editing and publishing.

From the first, Baker saw Tarnower as a rather stern and professional Marcus Welby type—a doctor who continued to treat a cross-section of patients through his hospital work and was widely known and respected throughout the county.

Baker knew Tarnower was a bachelor and that he lived in Purchase with his cook and landscape gardener. That was just about all he knew about him.

Several times he and his publisher, Eleanor

Rawson, were guests at Tarnower's house to savor gourmet dishes created by the doctor, but little about his personal life surfaced.

"He didn't offer any information, and I didn't ask," Baker said later. "He was not the kind of man you'd ask."

However, as a professional writer, Baker was always curious about people. At one of the dinner parties to which he had been invited to the elegant Tarnower house, Baker met Jean Harris, who was introduced to him as the headmistress of Madeira School.

One thing he learned from a brief talk with her was that she did not at all approve of the book that Baker was helping Tarnower write. She said that she thought a "diet book" cheapened Tarnower's image. It was strictly for the hoi polloi, she said.

Baker remembered her name, of course. She was that kind of person, who, even if she disapproved of one, was remembered.

But one odd incident did occur. When Baker had written the first chapter of the book, he took it to Tarnower's house on Purchase Street to let him read it. The idea was to submit a version for Tarnower's approval or even for suggestions for manuscript changes.

Tarnower read it and, according to Baker, called it excellent. Baker went on writing the next portion of the book, feeling he was on the right track.

Meanwhile, Tarnower had apparently had second thoughts. He called Baker and handed him a rewritten version of the chapter.

"We did some revisions on it," he told Baker. He never explained who "we" were, nor did Baker ask.

Reading the manuscript at home, Baker was appalled at the revision. It was, in his words, "terrible." It was the kind of "look-how-clever-I-am kind of writing" an amateur produces. It was, again in Baker's words, "amateurish, dreadful."

Baker met with Tarnower and told him what he thought about the revision. Tarnower handed the manuscript over to Baker. "Change it back to any way you want, Samm," Tarnower told him. "Line by line, if you want."

And Baker did so. From then on, he said, there were no revisions at all except for "technical" ones.

Baker was later asked if he had any ideas about who the "we" in Tarnower's statement referred to. "No," he said.

"Could it have been Jean Harris?" he was asked.

Baker refused to admit that, but the implications seemed obvious to him. He had good things to say about the doctor, however.

"I'll tell you one thing about Hi Tarnower," Baker told a friend later after the murder. "He really cared for people. Boy, did he care about making people well!"

Eleanor Rawson met the doctor several times at his home during the course of her work on the book.

"Tarnower was a workaholic," she said about him, "with a commanding presence and a very, very definite concept about what he wanted and didn't want."

When they talked about the book that he was working on, she said his attitude was that it would be a big money-maker. "He expected the book to succeed," she said. "He was a man accustomed to success."

Both she and Baker were fascinated by Tarnower's avid sportsmanship—particularly exemplified by the room full of trophies from his big-game hunting forays and his deep-sea fishing trips.

As a sensible man—and as a physician who understood the human body, the aging process, and the proper amount of stress it could take—he had given up the rigors of African safaris years ago, but still continued to hunt birds at favorite lodges in the Carolinas, Newfoundland and similar areas.

It was at the time Tarnower handed the list of acknowledgements to Baker that Tarnower's personal life seemed to surface a bit, so that a part almost became visible to those working closely with him on the book.

The list of acknowledgements began with this sentence:

"We are grateful to Jean Harris for her splendid assistance in the research and writing of this book. . . ."

And after that there was a long list of acknowledgements.

"There were 36 of them and she was at the top," Baker said. "I was stunned, and I said so to Tarnower."

Tarnower's response was that yes, Jean Harris *had* done some consulting with him at the start. And then he added that people on the staff at the Scarsdale Medical Center had "double-checked information" and had taken "the flood of phone calls that came in to the center."

Baker expressed his concern to his co-author about the large number of "helpers" and also about Jean Harris's "help."

"It's a private matter," Tarnower responded. "This is none of your concern, Samm. Whatever payment may be involved—well, I'll take care of that."

But the episode was puzzling to Baker. He could recall no direct contact with her, except the brief chat in which she had expressed her disapproval of the book he was working on, nor could he recall Tarnower ever mentioning her work on the manuscript. Unless, of course, she was the part of the "we" Tarnower mentioned during the incident of the abortive first chapter.

"Whatever she did for him, I never did know," Baker said.

Later on, the acknowledgements included the following:

"Suzanne van der Vreken, an imaginative nutritionist and artist, created many of the Gourmet and International recipes . . . ."

Of course Baker had met Tarnower's French-born cook and housekeeper, and knew that she had worked long and hard with him on the preparation of the dishes.

Once Tarnower had assured Baker that there would be no financial obligation to any of the list of people mentioned in the acknowledgements, he never mentioned the subject again. He was used to "authors" who did not write books as a profession; they did sometimes have different ideas about acknowledgements than professional authors did. So, disturbing as it was to Baker, it was not in any way a problem for him.

After the usual delays and problems, the book

was finally ready. It was published in January, 1979, but was in fact already in the book stores in December, 1978, where it began selling moderately well for the Christmas last-minute rush.

An instant success it was definitely *not*. The *Library Journal* immediately picked it to pieces, even before it was published.

"The Scarsdale diet probably can't hurt you, but whether it can make you lose one pound daily, as Tarnower claims, is another question," wrote the reviewer, Ruth E. Almeida, a librarian at the North County Library, Glen Burnie, Maryland.

"The diet is low in carbohydrates and fats and high in protein, producing a moderately ketonic affect. Lean meat, chicken, fish, vegetables, and fruit are the staples, with limited bread allowed.

"The book gives gourmet, international, and vegetarian variations as well as the basic diet. The warning to eat only until satisfied poses a discipline problem for the hungry dieter: with one grapefruit and a piece of dry toast for breakfast, the dieter may well overeat at lunch and dinner before his or her stomach registers 'full.'

"Also, some people may find that the 14-day period of the diet is not long enough to effect true behavior modification. No better or worse than most."

Whether or not the Glen Burnie library in Maryland ever purchased copies of the Scarsdale Diet book is not known, but certainly people who lived around the area paid out their $7.95 for the book—regardless of their librarian's dictum.

But her attack was gentle compared to others.

In facct, almost on publication, the Scarsdale Diet became a kind of *cause célèbre* in the world of nutrition. The controversy it stirred up among the medical people and nutrition experts who read it may have contributed to its interest among bookbuyers.

If there were plenty of things written about it—not all of those things were good.

Most of them were bad.

7.

The Controversy

The medical profession didn't wait very long to begin taking pot shots at the Scarsdale Diet. Although Hi Tarnower's book was scheduled for publication in January, 1979, galleys of the manuscript had been distributed and various articles on the diet were in preparation for some months before that.

One of the opening cannonades appeared in January, 1979, just when the book began appearing in book stores throughout the country. It was contained in *Vogue Magazine*'s January, 1979 issue.

From the medical profession: Dr. George L. Blackburn, director of nutritional support service at New England Deaconess Hospital in Boston, associate professor of surgery at Harvard Medical School. About the Scarsdale Diet, he wrote:

"It has a built-in factor for compliance—the medical term for doing what the physicians prescribes, because it spells out just what you're to eat for each meal for fourteen days. And the diet has an acceptable variety of foods that taste good."

However, if that appeared to be a statement of approval, Blackburn thought that the diet should have gone a step further. "While a diet is telling you what foods to eat, it should also direct the amounts to be eaten, particularly of calorie-dense items such as meat.

"For example, 'plenty of steak' is listed for dinner twice a week. That frequency is fine: but, to Amerians, plenty of steak can mean up to twelve, fourteen, even sixteen ounces. And, remember, steak registers eighty to ninety calories per ounce.

"It would be far better to weigh each meat portion across your kitchen scale and limit your serving to about four ounces after cooking."

Blackburn also commented on the fact that the Scarsdale Diet plan prohibited the use of any vegetable oil or fat, as well as butter, for such food preparation as cooking vegetables or dressing salad. Thus, polyunsaturated fat was eliminated from the diet. The fat allowed was the saturated, cholesterol-bearing animal fat contained in meat, cheese, and eggs.

Dropping out polyunsaturated fats while eating meat and cold cuts, Blackburn said, was actually moving in the opposite direction from current nutritional advice, which recommended that dietary oil and fat should be largely the polyunsaturated kind.

He also disliked the inclusion of cold cuts in the diet. "Cold cuts are high in sodium, high in fat, and relatively low in nutrients; not a very good protein source. They don't begin to compare in value with similar portions of fish, lean meat, cottage cheese, or cooked navy beans."

Cold cuts like boiled ham, spiced luncheon meat, and minced ham did sometimes have as much as 50 percent more calories, half to two-thirds less protein, three times as much fat, and five to twenty times as much sodium as similar portions of lean beef, fish, and chicken. He pointed out that cooked beans and cottage cheese are low-calorie, low-fat foods with protein values only one-half to one-third lower than the meat/fish/chicken group.

Blackburn argued against one of the general beliefs stated in the Scarsdale Diet: that foods high in complex carbohydrates—that is, starches—are very fattening and must be avoided; and that bread, potatoes, rice and beans are considered off limits in a weight-control diet.

Thus, the Scarsdale diet holds carbohydrates to a minimum—no alcohol, no sugar, and only one thin slice of toasted protein bread each day, with an extra slice on fish and egg dinner menus.

"We really must unglue that notion," Blackburn contended. "There is nothing uniquely fattening about a carbohydrate except that in one form—sugar—it tastes so good we may overeat. But there should be a definite place in the diet for the legumes, such as beans, peas, and lentils. They give you fiber, they satisfy hunger, and they give excellent nutritional value, including protein."

Blackburn attacked another instruction in the Scarsdale diet: that the combinations of foods listed for each meal should be strictly observed. He noted that the case against substitutions was provided not for the purpose of burning body fat faster, but for the purpose of providing a balance of nutrients and giving appetizing variety to meals.

"Being on a low-carbohydrate diet is not going to burn off fat," Blackburn argued. "Eating fewer calories and spending more energy than you take in is the only way to get your body to consume its fat stores. There certainly is nothing magic that will enhance fatburning in any diet."

It wasn't only Blackburn who had reservations about the Scarsdale Diet. Dr. Peter D. Vash of Los Angeles had a different reaction. "This diet," he was quoted as saying in *McCall's Magazine* of June, 1979, "although most likely safe and probably minimally effective for a short term, does little to educate the obese, overweight person in basic nutritional principles. The Scarsdale Diet does not address itself to the more fundamental underlying emotional issues for which overeating and weight gain may be but a symptom."

Dr. Paul De Vore of Hyattsville, Maryland, pointed out: "One of the hazards of this diet is the vagueness of the portion sizes. It is generally agreed that it is very important for the dieter to restructure his eating patterns along the line of smaller portion sizes. Obviously, the Scarsdale Diet cannot accomplish that goal because it ignores the concept of portion size altogether."

"Eating as much as you want is bad advice for many dieters," another doctor stated. "There are a lot of calories in steak and chicken, and people will over-indulge."

"Many of my patients," said one doctor, "if urged to start the Scarsdale Diet, would gain weight without difficulty. The amount of food prescribed is far beyond what the majority of them can eat and still lose weight."

"Our body needs no more than 1.2 to 1.4 grams of protein per kilogram of ideal body weight—any excess becomes fat," said Dr. Tomas Garchitorena of Old Bethpage, New York.

Dr. Sami Hashim of St. Luke's Hospital Center and Columbia University, a nutritionist, asserted that Tarnower's approach—which declared that dieting success was owing to a metabolic change brought on by the restricting of carbohydrates—"had not been subjected to scientific scrutiny."

"The initial weight loss is due to the loss of water and electrolytes such as minerals in the body," Hashim pointed out. "And if weight loss continues thereafter it must be due to a reduced number of calories compared to the individual's intake prior to going on the diet."

Dr. Francis Vincent of Jacksonville, Illinois, said: "Once the dieter chooses to return to unrestricted foods, the predictable rebound is often devastating (especially in spirit) and will undoubtedly propel the participant to levels of weight higher than that occupied prior to dieting."

And Dr. David G. Johnson, chief of endocrinology at the University of Arizona Health Sciences Center in Tucson, wrote: "Weight loss through special chemical interactions of foods just doesn't exist. People lose fat through negative calorie balance—spending more energy than they take in as food."

Johnson said that the Scarsdale diet appeared metabolically and nutritionally sound, although there was no chemical magic about it. On the 1,000 to 1,200 calories a day the Scarsdale Diet provided, when meat intake was kept moderate, "most people should lose one to three pounds a

109

week."

Nevertheless, the point most doctors emphasized was this: the bottom line in weight control is that once you take fat off, only permanent changes in eating habits will *keep it off*. The majority of dieters usually regain the weight they've lost, which historically accounts for the fact that dieters go from one diet to another as soon as they find themselves overweight once again.

A balanced diet is important, but a balanced life style is even *more* essential to health, wellbeing, vitality. For those of us who have been doing it wrong, as indicated by the need for a weight loss diet, it may be time to consider change.

"This involves not just change in the way of eating," Blackburn wrote in the *Vogue* article mentioned, "but change in the way of thinking about oneself, including exercise and relaxation on a regular basis. Without brand-new living habits, weight loss and dieting just isn't going to work for you."

Consumer Guide Magazine had plenty to say. Their story quoted Philip L. White, Sc.D., of the American Medical Association in his opinion of the diet and its essentials.

"This diet is extremely rigid," White told the editors of the *Guide*. "The dieter has few decisions to make and these are minor. This very rigidity encourages compliance for a while. There is no 'metabolic miracle' performed, just tight control of what you eat."

In their evaluation of the diet, the magazine wrote:

"Great Dr. Stillman's ghost!" They were referring to Samm Sinclair Baker's earlier collaborator, Dr. Irwin Maxwell Stillman. "The Scarsdale Diet is much like those 'grapefruit diets' passed from hand to hand in offices and beauty parlors. .

"It is a slightly modified version of the later Stillman Diet since fruits and vegetables are allowed. Highly unbalanced, this diet allows you to eat foods from one major group—dairy—only on two days of the week: at Thursday's and Friday's lunch.

"Actually," the magazine continued, "it should be called the Scarsdale Mystery Diet. The mystery is how Tarnower and Baker claim that their basic diet is 43 percent protein, 22.5 percent fat, and 34.5 percent carbohydrates.

"These percentages are obtained from the total calories consumed every day, but Tarnower and Baker don't specify how many actual daily calories the diet aims for. More importantly, the diet is purposely vague as to quantity of foods eaten. The only place you might derive quantities is in the Gourmet Recipe section since each recipe indicates how many persons it should serve.

"As if that weren't error enough, Tarnower and Baker commit an even heavier error when they tell us the Scarsdale diet is NOT a fad diet and that it is intended to modify behavior.

"Now, anyone who has ever studied behavior of fat people knows that 'plenty of steak' indicates a far larger quantity of beef to them than it does to lean people. When the authors tell the reader to eat as much as he or she wants 'as long as you avoid overloading your stomach to the point of discomfort,' they are displaying astonishing naïveté."

The report went on to castigate Tarnower on his statement in the book that there is "magic" in protein. Every individual needs protein, the editors admitted, but most people need only so much. All protein beyond the minimum is not only money lost but carbohydrate gained, since that is exactly what excess protein is converted to by the body!

Concluding the report, the magazine stated:

"The only commendable part of the diet is that it emphasizes polyunsaturated oils and limits saturated fats as it cuts back on total daily fat intake. Other than that, and its rigidity, which may help some, the Scarsdale diets are a throwback to a time when dieters were less enlightened.

"To effectively lose weight and keep it off, you need a diet for a lifetime. Any diet that says it is designed for only two weeks' use is faddish, foolish, and forgettable."

In spite of all those criticisms, and in spite of the medical and nutritional societies' stand, and in spite of dozens of other criticisms as well, the Scarsdale Diet became the sensation of 1979.

The book did not quickly become a best-seller. It took a month or two, but when it got there, it stayed there. In 1979-80, the book was on the best-seller list for 44 weeks.

By the time the hardback sales were over and the book was in paperback, the title had racked up sales figures of 750,000. It had gone through 23 printings in the first edition from Rawson, Wade.

Bantam Books bought the paperback rights once it was evident that the hardback sale was a success. About 3,000,000 paperbacks were in print, with 2,250,000 already sold at the time of Tarnower's death.

There were plenty of satisfied customers.

John Mariana, who had been appointed food critic for the Home Section of the *New York Times* in January, 1979, decided to try out the Scarsdale Diet in order not to, as he put it, "inflate to the size of Orson Welles."

He kept a record of the 14 days of the Scarsdale Diet—and had fun writing it up. His reflections probably duplicate the feelings of many of the people who took the diet.

Here are some excerpts from his "record:"

"Day 1: I begin the first of 14 breakfasts of grapefruit, black coffee and protein toast. Not so bad. The toast actually is kind of nutty-tasting. Some cold cuts for lunch, a tasteless orange tomato. We play a little tennis that evening in the full flush of health and hunger, then have a nice broiled porgy for dinner. . . .

"Day 2: . . .[I] enjoy a terrific barbecued sirloin steak from Suzanne's Supermarket in Chester Heights. This diet isn't unbearable, I think, and I've already dropped two pounds.

"Day 3: I must do a [food] review this week. . so I choose a restaurant I've already visited once, meaning I can order simply and merely taste everyone else's food. I gnawed my lamb chops like a Neanderthal back from the hunt. Across the table my dinner companions are polishing off french fries and onion rings, followed by various pies and ice creams. One has drunk three beers. I'm beginning to feel like a character out of "Oliver Twist."

"Day 4: I am encouraged to see I have actually lost four pounds, so I celebrate with an extra portion of carrot sticks at lunch. . . . My father-in-law comes over tonight, and my wife makes an extraordinary dinner of stuffed cabbage. . . . as I try to cope with the dreaded 'Friday night diet dinner'—two scrambled eggs, cottage cheese and cooked cabbage—a combination I believe was created by the chef on Devil's Island.

"Day 5: The neighbors have invited us for dinner. . . . We stand around drinking Perrier with a large slice of lime. . . . The main course is chicken casserole, of which I eat three forkfuls. I almost faint again when a hostess brings out a carrot cake with vanilla icing. I . . . eat two bites. That night I dream that I die and go to purgatory, where a satanic-looking Dr. Tarnower tells me I must stay on this diet for 22,000 years before getting into heaven. . . .

"Day 6: . . . . I have come to regard tomatoes as enemies, and look askance at all vegetarians.

"Day 7: Disaster! I forgot it was my brother-in-law's anniversary, and I promised to take him to Amerigo's, a restaurant in the Bronx I'd recently given three stars to and a place that serves the most sublime pasta dishes around. . . . I'm miserable; my brother-in-law . . . eats melon and prosciutto, tortellini in brodo, fettucine Alfredo, veal marsala and cappucino and whipped cream. I eat chicken broth, a wonderful veal chop and broccoli . . . . The wine tonight is La Romanee-St. Vivant '73. I sip one glass, very slowly. I actually feel drunk when I finish it. Then the coup de grace: an anniversary cake from Dumas Patisserie! Chocolate cream at that. I look at my wife. . . . We split a small slice. It's the greatest thing I've ever tasted in my whole life. . . .

"Day 8: A week and eight pounds gone. It's all downhill from here, but that nutty protein toast is beginning to taste like cardboard and those wretched grapefruit taste vile. . . . That night . . . we . . . eat out: The Oyster Bar in Grand Central. Our mackeral and wolf fish are perfectly broiled, crisp on the outside, fragrant with lemon, washed down with a Diet Pepsi—a drink I've always hated but have now made peace with.

"Day 9: I'm constantly starving, even though my stomach has obviously shrunk. But the food on this diet is so banal that I can't even bring myself to finish what little is on my plate. I can't take another spoonful of fruit salad. I never want to look another cold fish in the eye. . . .

"Day 10: . . . .I'm beginning to feel like Charlie Chaplin in "Modern Times' when he is force-fed by machine.

"Day 12: Tonight I must attend a dinner at the Culinary Institute of America in honor of Don Zacharia, owner of Westchester's finest wine store, Zachy's in Scarsdale. I'm told there will be a six-course meal and 55 wines!. . . I confine myself to taking no more than a sip of those wines I've never before encountered—maybe 20 or so . . . .

"Day 13: . . . People say I look like I lost weight. . . . My wife has gone off the diet, having gotten down to the weight she was in college. She looks great. But she insists on eating Haagen-Dazs chocolate ice cream in the same room with me, a cruel streak I never knew she possessed.

"Day 14: . . . This is a tough one. By accident we stumble upon a street fair in Pelham, and like

St. Francis of Assisi trying to avoid temptation by throwing himself into a thornbush, I duck into an art gallery rather than be lured by the food stalls outside. . . . Cola, cola, everywhere, nor any drop to drink! But what am I to hamburger, and hamburger to me? I have survived! Not even a cold chicken dinner bothers me now. I go to bed a thinner man—by 13 pounds.''

Mariana wound up his article:

''I cheated, sure, but not much. I hated every minute, but it worked. And the dread, the utter dread of ever having to go through such gastronomic trauma again will keep me chaste to the table. I am, once again John Mariana, restaurant critic, at your service and light on his feet. Bring on your pecan pies, your clams Posillipo, your carre d'agneau! But bring on small portions, please.''

Supermarkets began pinning up signs reading: ''Get Your Scarsdale Medical Diet Celery Here.'' Restaurants ranging from Beverly Hills' ultrafashionable Ma Maison to the New York area's Zum Zum fast-food chain began offering Scarsdale meals. At Goodman's Restaurant in the Chicago suburb of Highland Park, owner Bob Goodman and his partner-son Steve both went on the diet and liked the results so much they put it on their regular bill of fare.

And in the House of Representatives House Speaker Tip O'Neill tried the diet and lost 40 pounds! ''That diet,'' he said, ''is a thing of beauty!''

In fashionable restaurants like Manhattan's ''21'' Club and Washington's Duke Zeibert's, an inordinate number of customers appeared to be feasting—or fasting, as the case might actually be—on the same simply prepared dish.

There was a lot of fish—if it happened to be Monday night.

There was a lot of beef—if it happened to be Tuesday.

There was a lot of lamb—if it happened to be Wednesday.

Everybody seemed to be following the Scarsdale Diet.

"Some socialites with no weight problems at all are following it simply because it is chic," wrote *Time Magazine*.

"Everyone's been on it," declared a Chicago hostess, Donna ("Sugar") Rautbord. "I believe its appeal is its popularity."

Even Craig Claiborne, the *New York Times* gourmet expert, liked it. In fact, he was invited to Tarnower's house in Purchase where he ate a gourmet diet meal prepared by Suzanne van der Vreken.

He visited the estate, and even commented on Tarnower's vegetable garden in the story that appeared in the *Times*. "The Tarnower garden, incidentally, is supposed to be one of the great sights of summer."

Claiborne mentioned Tarnower's cook. "Suzanne who contributed numerous 'gourmet and Continental' recipes for the diet book, achieves interest in her foods by using a variety of condiments including soy sauce, lemon juice, vinegar, onions and other assorted well-flavored vegetables such as tomatoes and green pepper."

And he said what had been said many years before—by the ancient Greeks about life in general:

"The important thing in dieting [Tarnower]

observed, is to eat in moderation."

And he quoted Tarnower: "Most people don't know what to eat. Or rather, what to avoid. If you are trying to lose weight, you should avoid butter, margarine, all fats, oils and fancy desserts like sin."

It was the dietist's contention that food could be palatable and tasty with a total absence of fats, Claiborne wrote.

"Taste everything and eat nothing," Tarnower was supposed to have said to a traveling companion making a tour through France. "That," Claiborne wrote, "is, I suspect, a slight exaggeration of the Tarnower philosophy, better expressed elsewhere in the book. Act like a gourmet—respect and enjoy the food that is placed before you and dine on small portions; and not like a gourmand, consuming willy-nilly and thoughtlessly, every morsel that is placed on your plate."

And Claiborne also remarked: "One of the many strong points of the Tarnower diet is that while it stresses a total absence [visible] of fats and rich desserts, it offers an abundance of well-rounded and interesting recipes, varied and international in scope. It makes excellent use of such diverse flavors and ingredients as oregano, lemon juice, capers, mushrooms, bean sprouts, nuts and so on. It is, in fact, a Scarsdale version of cuisine minceur."

He also wrote: "The Scarsale diet could be rechristened 'The Common Sense Book of Losing Weight.' Its principles are simple and sound. You avoid fats and sugar and high-calorie snacks, peanuts and other seemingly 'trivial' between-meal foods."

In fact, even *Consumer Guide* was not so rough on the Tarnower diet as it was on the Atkins diet, which it did not recommend at all. But it gave two stars—on a sliding downward scale of four stars as tops and one star as bottom—to the Scarsdale diet.

It added this admonition in evaluation of the diet:

"A high-protein diet is an effective way to lose fat, but an extraordinarily high intake of protein also results in a high intake of cholesterol. In addition, such a diet can be used only by people who have no evidence of kidney disease.

"Even for people in good health, plenty of water is necessary to wash away the ketone bodies left in the blood as a result of the mobilization and incomplete burning of fat.

"Such a diet is not for pregnant women or anyone with gout (unless specially adapted). It can be used by diabetics only with modification and a doctor's consultation.

"A high-protein diet may cause fatigue, which can be remedied by a glass of orange juice. As in starvation fasting, a high-protein diet causes bad breath . . . ."

Everyone seemed to worry about the diet except the people who wanted to diet.

And the people who wanted to diet liked it so much they made a best-seller out of it. The hit was so big that, shortly afterward, Tarnower's publishers wanted him to go ahead with another one, and they designated Baker to approach him with a proposal to that effect.

"I suggested a follow-up to the diet book," Baker said, "with a special angle to it—answers to questions perhaps—and he said he would

119

think about it."

Finally, around January, 1980, Baker brought up the subject again with Tarnower. The doctor told Baker he was a little uncertain about it. Was he thinking of Jean Harris's opinion of the diet book?

"You know," he said, "I'm a pretty good cardiologist, but now nobody really thinks about me in that way. I don't want to be known as a diet doctor!"

Tarnower mentioned the fact that he had been thinking about a book on longevity. "It would be a fountain-of-youth kind of book, a philosophical type of book about my own thoughts on medicine."

Baker was not enthusiastic. "I don't think I would be interested in that kind of book. Why don't you write that one yourself?"

"I'm a doctor, not a writer."

"But you have a good turn of phrase, you write extremely well." That was praise indeed from a writer of Baker's professional status.

Tarnower, according to Baker, smiled, and said, "Well, don't be surprised then, if I write a book on longevity, Samm. But also, don't be surprised if I come back to you with your idea on another diet book."

But of course he never did.

8

The Breach

It is not known exactly what brought about the actual beginning of the end of the long-standing relationship between Hi Tarnower and Jean Harris. For some fourteen years, ever since they had met in Philadelphia, the two had been frequent dinner companions, spent time together on weekends, tramped golf courses together, had even gone on prolonged vacations together.

Both individuals had always been extremely private people—austere and aloof about their personal lives.

"You could never get him to talk about any women in his life," one acquaintance of Tarnower's noted.

"She didn't seem to have any personal life to speak of," said a friend of Jean Harris's.

Yet even after her move to Virginia in July, 1977, she continued to spend her weekends at the home she had bought in Mahopac, apparently driving down to the Purchase home of Tarnower throughout the year.

Obviously the physical proximity which had tended to weld their relationship together was no longer able to sustain the union. Dinners together at the Purchase house during the week were now out of the question—in fact, physically impossible. Yet on weekends things could be the same as they had always been.

But Hi Tarnower's life did not consist only of weekends. He wanted companionship and friends around throughout the week. He was not a man who tolerated a situation that did not correspond to his wishes. If Jean Harris could not be there during the week, there was one obvious solution.

Tarnower simply sought out someone else to substitute for her during the nights when she could not be there with him. He did not have far to search. There were plenty of women around him who would gladly fill the breach.

By the time Tarnower's Scarsdale Diet book was being written, there must have been a cooling off between the two. According to people who knew them both—a small, select circle of friends and relatives—their relationship was now beginning to unravel.

The first indication of the split was Jean Harris's sudden action in returning Tarnower's ring. He had given her a beautiful, expensive diamond ring that some who saw it said was valued at somewhere in the neighborhood of $50,000. Now, sometime during this crucial period of their relationship, she gave it back.

Did she mean for him to take it back without a struggle? Was it a ploy to force him to give her the ring again on condition he marry her? Did she think she could manipulate him into marriage?

If Jean Harris did return the ring in an attempt to bring about a marriage proposal, her gamble did not pay off. She wound up without the ring and without the man who had given it to her.

And if she did indeed use the ring to force his
hand, she had not read her man right, had been
deluding herself about him for the years they
had been together.

Some said, in fact, that the two principals of
the relationship, so different in attitudes and
mores, had always been on a collision course
from the start. The natures of the two were
simply such that they could not be smoothly
compatible no matter how hard each of them
worked at it.

Tarnower was an avowed bachelor. He had
decided a long time ago never to marry. "He was
totally committed to medicine," one friend said,
"and did not think it would be fair to marry any
woman and have children. But he was square
about it with the women who were his companions."

The opinion stated could well have been the
truth. By nature, Tarnower was a workaholic, a
man who lived for his profession, a man who
lived to care for people under his medical
supervision.

At the same time he was a man who loved his
leisure, his privacy, and who continued to travel,
play golf, hunt and fish, and involve himself in
recreation as much as ever.

Complicated man that he was, his actions
were not. He liked the company of beautiful
women, people of good breeding, with good
taste, with a sense of civilization. That was the
reason he had taken up with Jean Harris in the
first place. She *belonged* to the milieu. She
suited him—her background, her attitudes, her
ability to enjoy and revel in the better things in

life.

They were, in fact, admirably suited to one another on the surface. The one basic and fundamental difference lay in their beliefs and convictions, their very psyches.

Jean Harris believed in the old-fashioned virtues—and these included marriage.

Hi Tarnower, quite simply, did not believe in marriage—at least for himself.

Tarnower knew after he had known her for a very short time, how Jean Harris felt about marriage, the simple verities of her moral tenets. Tarnower had apparently never pretended to be interested in marriage. He was too honest and too straightforward to practice that kind of deception. Presumably he had laid it on the line to her, warning her how he felt. But she must have decided that her beliefs would make no difference in their relationship.

On the other hand, Jean Harris might not have been quite so honest with herself as Tarnower was with himself. She may have decided that although he was a confirmed bachelor *now,* he might *someday* change his mind. If she thought that, she certainly was hoodwinking herself. Once she became acquainted with him and understood what made up his character, she must have realized that he was never going to change. He was a dedicated man—dedicated to a single lifestyle. That lifestyle obviously could not incorporate marriage.

Besides, he continually saw other women. "He had tremendous sex appeal," said one male friend. "Women were strongly attracted to him." Most of the people around Tarnower knew it. Tarnower was discreet in his relationships, but in spite of discretion, most everyone knew that he was a confirmed swinger. Jean Harris certainly knew that.

"He had a reputation as a chaser," said a doctor from White Plains who knew him. "He liked young women, some in their twenties."

Another friend amplified a bit on that statement. "It was a case of one woman at a time. He did not play the field."

Consistent with all the other aspects of his life, this would not have caused a conflict for Tarnower. But perhaps there was conflict in the mind of Jean Harris. If so, that conflict had very probably existed there from the beginning of their friendship and, as the split between her ideals and her actions continued to widen, she would begin to suffer from the consquences of the unresolved conflict in her psyche.

Could she actually have been one person on the surface and another person within? The stern disciplinarian on the outside who believed in adhering to the rigors of society, without deviation, yet the woman inside who believed in living a double life—one life right and proper, the other life informal and involved?

Her basic beliefs and her basic actions were constantly in direct conflict. When she began to sense that she was hurting herself by what she was doing, it is quite likely that she tried to change the circumstances. Perhaps she tried to persuade Tarnower to marry her. According to acquaintances, she did almost everything she could to convince him that they would be the perfect husband and wife.

But of course it did no good. Tarnower apparently ignored her psychological assaults on him. He was an astute diplomat and knew when to give in, when to argue, and when to call time out. And she was able to play that game, too.

At first she relented in her attacks, played a waiting game, and permitted the relationship to continue on the way it had begun. Very soon, however, her own frustration and guilt began to erode her personality from within. Associates noticed that she was subject to sudden rages.

"She was very intense, very intense," one student at Madeira observed of her three years there. "Even the littlest thing seemed to set her off." Others said that she was given to unexplainable emotional outbursts. A *Washington Post* story revealed that "she had a violent temper and would shout and scream at the students."

Since these blow-ups were confined to moments of extreme stress, Jean Harris generally evoked the image of a serene, well-controlled, soft-spoken, genteel woman of the world. It was this image that most of those in her professional life remembered.

Fame can do strange things to men and women. Decent, easy-going people can become cruel tyrants overnight. Soft-spoken people can become shouting, raving maniacs. Modest people can become egomaniacs.

Curiously, almost nothing appeared to happen to Hi Tarnower when his diet book became a big best-seller. He remained the austere, intellectual, hard-working doctor.

Samm Sinclair Baker said he was "the type of man you'd think was the chairman of General Motors. He was," Baker noted, "warm but remote."

Tarnower was, nonetheless, now famous. To Jean Harris, the sudden escalation of Tarnower's name to that of public "personality" must have been a bitter pill to swallow.

Jean Harris had always believed in maintaining what is now called a "low profile" in life. Fame was equivalent to notoriety. She did not believe in it.

She had always loathed the idea of Tarnower's "diet book" from the first moment. It is probable that she had privately recommended that he not do it.

Her attitude was quite appropriate for the headmistress of a private girls' school. It was quite appropriate indeed for any person in the academic world. A "diet book" was essentially a "non-book"—that is, a simple how-to manual for fat folks. Books were classics of literature: *Lorna Doone, Wuthering Heights, Jane Eyre, Pride and Prejudice,* the works of George Sand, Jane Austen, and the like.

How appalled she must have been to see the steady climb of the Scarsdale Diet book on the best-seller lists! How frustrated she must have inwardly become to think that the entire country now knew of the man she was so intimate with—and knew him as the author of a diet manual that was making millions of dollars in sales!

But the most miserable thought of all must have been that she had been against the book from the beginning. Secondarily, that she had failed to persuade Tarnower not to go ahead with it. Always in the back of her mind, she must have thought that perhaps Tarnower was thinking even now how she had tried to dissuade him from the book which was bringing him fame and fortune, even though, of course, he modestly wanted to be remembered as a "good cardiologist" rather than a "diet doc."

Tarnower's new celebrity status might have made him even more adamant about remaining a bachelor, and this could have caused a problem in his relationship with Jean Harris.

After Jean Harris had moved to Virginia, their arguments must have become more and more intense and protracted. Friends reported that they sometimes quarreled loudly. This was unusual, for the two had maintained such a discreet and successful relationship for so long.

According to some reports, Jean Harris began to shift her tactics. She had always known that Tarnower saw other women. Now she began to question him.

What had he done during the week? Whom had he seen? What other woman was he with?

Jean Harris had never before been bothered by the "other women" in his life. She had accepted them—at least on the surface—as part of the Tarnower package.

But now, sometime around 1977, during the years when she was making the break and planning her move to Virginia, she may have experienced feelings of jealousy.

According to one friend, Jean Harris herself had replaced an earlier companion of the doctor's. The woman had accompanied him on an Asian trip sometime in the mid 1960s.

"When the time came that Jean realized she too was being replaced," the friend said, "she became possessive."

Dr. Herman Tarnower, 69, bachelor cardiologist, celebrated for <u>The Scarsdale Diet</u>, connoisseur of good food, fine wine, and attractive women, fatally shot in his bedroom.

Policeman leaving the Tarnower home after the fatal shooting. Dr. Tarnower was the creator of its Japanese-modern design.

*Jean Struven Harris, 56, divorcee, headmistress of the
Madeira school, about to enter the Harrison, New York
court where she was arraigned for the murder of her companion of 14 years.*

Jean Struven Harris, whose residence was in McLean, Virginia, directed to a car after leaving the police station where she was booked. To her students she preached the importance of a stout and loving heart.

"I have been through so much hell with him. I loved him very much. I had it." Jean Struven Harris uttered these words to police shortly after the diet doctor died.

One acquaintance told of a time Harris had driven up from Virginia unannounced, and rushed into Tarnower's house. There she had run through all the rooms searching for evidence that would prove he had another woman there.

According to the report, Tarnower was angry at her attitude, and ordered her never to do anything like that again.

"You're seeing other women!" she cried.

"Of course I'm seeing other women!" he retorted, unable to fathom her attitude about something that had never bothered her before.

She began weeping.

Tarnower, it was said, didn't bother to comfort her. Instead he told her that she would have to act like a lady or get out of the house.

Apparently that kind of tough talk appealed to Jean Harris's battered psyche. She must have known that if he spoke roughly that way to her, he must care a geat deal about the way she felt about him. He *couldn't* simply ignore her. Thus, her logic told her, he *did* care for her.

A psychologist who studied the relationship noted that Jean Harris may well have been—in her own mind, unknown perhaps to herself—testing Tarnower's opinion of her. Had he broken down and comforted her, she would immediately have set out to manipulate him into giving up his "other women friends," or at least have made him promise to do so. At least, that is apparently what her subconscious intention had been.

But when he had scolded her like an errant child, she had immediately relented and apologized for her outburst, resulting in a return to the status quo.

It wasn't all that status quo with Tarnower, apparently. He seemed sick of all the squabbling. In fact, he may have begun to get sick of her. How many times had they played that psychological cat and mouse game together?

Without question, Tarnower did inform her that he would go out with whom he pleased, and that she would have nothing to do with his choice of friends.

Several times during their arguments, it is reported, she stalked out on him. But she always came back, and she always would come back. When she returned, he always took her back. From his point of view, she had never really left; he had no reason to drop her. He had not even thought of severing relations with her.

Not, that is, until the winter after his book had made his name a household word—and then he might have considered it. No one knows.

But the situation was changing. There was a definite breach in the Tarnower/Harris relationship. A new element had been introduced.

"I remember seeing him with a blonde in her early forties at a party last December," said one close friend of Tarnower's, an advertising executive, referring to the winter of 1979-80, the winter that the Scarsdale Diet had become world-famous. The friend, who knew Jean Harris, had been used to seeing her with Tarnower.

"I was startled to see him with a different woman," the friend continued. He sensed a subtle difference in Tarnower. The acquaintance, an advertising executive, was curious, but did not actively pursue obvious questions that rose in his own mind.

"Apparently there had definitely been some

change in his relationship with Mrs. Harris. Usually you would see him with Mrs. Harris. They went out together for years.''

Although the ad man did not learn the woman's name the night he saw Tarnower out with her, he did remember that she appeared to be an attractive, vivacious blonde. He was under the impression that she was of Scandinavian descent.

A White Plains doctor, an associate of Tarnower's, remembered that he too had seen Tarnower out with a blonde woman who was not Jean Harris, had in fact seen her with him off and on for several years before the diet book hit the best-seller list.

He recalled that during the time the book was making publishing history, he began to see Tarnower out with the younger woman as a more or less regular thing. But he did see Jean Harris, too.

''The relationship with Mrs. Harris, meanwhile, slowed down though.''

One odd aspect of the situation, according to the White Plains physician, was as if Tarnower selected his women—alternating between Jean Harris and the mysterious ''new companion''—in the same way he might alternate his wardrobe between white tie and tails and informal jacket and tie.

Jean Harris would appear with Tarnower at ''fancy'' gatherings, and the ''other woman'' would appear at the less formal, more ''common'' get-togethers.

It was as if the younger woman ''was not socially acceptable to these fancy people,'' as the White Plains doctor put it.

Then, abruptly, something changed in the relationship between Tarnower and Jean Harris. Tarnower began showing up at elegant gatherings with the "other woman."

"He came out of the closet, so to speak, and she got to go to the fancy parties."

Other acquaintances reported the same facts. It has been estimated that as many as 200 people were quite aware that Tarnower was "courting" two different women. It was not unusual for Tarnower to have either Jean Harris or the other woman walking with him when he played golf at the Century Country Club in Purchase.

"The doctor appeared to enjoy the companionship of one as much as the other," this friend said. "At least that's the way it looked on the surface."

The obvious "doppleganger" situation in Tarnower's personal life took on an amusing aspect. Acquaintances began to note a seasonal change in the doctor's escorts. Jean Harris began to be called Tarnower's "summer girlfriend"—obviously, when school was out and she was free, while the "other woman" became known as the "winter girlfriend."

Those close to Tarnower said that there was no secret in the fact that Tarnower split his interest equally between the two women, and both were described as "extremely lovely, well-poised ladies."

There was at least twenty years' difference in age between the rivals for his affections. Jean Harris was in her fifties, the other woman was in her thirties. And Tarnower, of course, was in his sixties!

According to those who knew Tarnower, it

was obvious that the younger woman was winning out over the older one. Graceful, almost tremulously sincere, she would hover over the cardiologist almost protectively, anticipating his every wish and direction, smilingly catering to his polite, almost courtly and frequent requests to do all the little tasks and errands one usually performs for oneself.

Psychologists say that men subsconsciously select companions of the opposite sex. That is, if a man divorces one woman, the woman he chooses for his wife the second time around may well exhibit all the basic qualities of his first.

The same, psychologists say, is true of lovers.

Psychologists would have found that Hi Tarnower's choice of escorts was well within the parameters of that theory, on the surface at least.

Both women were blondes.

Both women had blue eyes.

Both women were beautiful.

Both women were slim.

Both women were divorcees.

Both women had two children.

Both women were bringing up their children on their own.

Both women were obviously swept up in adoration for the doctor.

Both women seemed to resemble one another in that they might have come from the same background.

But there were important temperamental differences.

It was these differences in temperament that brought about the final solution to the triangle that had so quietly developed.

We know two angles of the triangle. What about the third?

9

The Other

Marjorie Brundage was born in 1943 in Ossining, New York. Her mother and father, according to Ossining Village Clerk Lester Kimball, apparently came from Manhattan.

But they didn't stay in Ossining too long. The neighborhood where Marjorie grew up was described as having been a "bit drab." Her mother did not stay married to Marjorie's father long, and after the divorce married William H. Tirrell, who became Marjorie's father through most of her younger years.

After moving from Ossining, the family went to the Green Knolls section of Eastchester. It was there that Marjorie went to grammar school. Soon the Tirrells moved to a house on Edgemont Road, off Ardsley Road, in a somewhat elegant house that would now market at about $175,000.

Marjorie went to Edgemont High School, and began to use her middle name rather than "Marjorie," which she might have thought a bit common. Her middle name was Lynne.

Lynne Brundage was a fresh, untouched, charming young girl. Even after the World War II years, she was what would be called "the girl next door," rather than a "femme fatale."

She was an uncomplicated, smiling, lovely, happy young girl, without guile, without sophistication, without any of the twists and turns that can make a personality irritating and yet fascinating.

She was not an intellect. In fact, she was never a natural student, or even an average one. She did not flunk out, but she had none of the intellectual genius of many of her contemporaries.

After her graduation from Edgemont High, she was enrolled in Endicott Junior College in Beverley, Massachusetts. Endicott now costs about $4,150 a year, and is known as "a rich girl's school, and for girls who aren't very good students."

The school offers a medical secretarial program, but not a medical technician course. Quite probably, Lynne Brundage was enrolled in the medical secretarial program. However, after one year at Endicott, she decided to drop out. She had met a man in Boston named Nicholas Tryforos. When he asked her to marry him, she accepted, and they were wedded in a double religious ceremony—Greek Orthodox and Protestant.

Nick Tryforos soon became the co-owner of a florist establishment called the Tryforos and Pernice Flower Shop in Edgemont.

"Lynne was a good mother to her two children, and a good wife," said one Edgemont resident. "She often helped her husband in the flower shop."

Nevertheless, the marriage, which had started out so beautifully, began to go to pieces in the early 1970s. In 1972, Lynne Tryforos, still a married woman, got a job at the Scarsdale

Medical Center.

She was not a nurse, but, through her medical secretarial course, she became a secretary-assistant to several of the doctors at the Center. Hi Tarnower was one of them.

In 1976, her marriage to Tryforos fell apart, and she obtained a divorce. She and her two daughters, then aged 10 and 14, moved into a Scarsdale house near the Center. It was at about this time that Lynne Tryforos apparently became a more or less alternate "date" for Hi Tarnower.

Her work at the Center was apparently divided among various functions. When he was working on the diet book with Tarnower, Samm Sinclair Baker said he saw Lynne Tryforos give machine-type tests to patients, and another source of information said she originally took care of all electrocardiograms. In New York State, certification is not required for a person administering electrocardiogram tests. The job could have been part of her functions there.

In any case, she was working for several of the doctors at that time, and had not yet settled in as Hi Tarnower's "office manager" as she has been described from about 1979 on. In that position, it was said, she appeared to "program" Tarnower's every moment, even preparing his lunch each day, which usually consisted of yogurt mixed with fresh fruit and walnuts.

At first, when the newly divorced woman became available for social dinners and events, Tarnower may have dated her a few times. That was even before Jean Harris moved to Virginia.

But when Jean Harris left for Madeira School, things changed to a more obvious degree. In fact, friends of Tarnower's have said that her sudden absence in Tarnower's social life created a kind of vacuum. She had always been at his beck and call. Working in Manhattan and later in Connecticut, she had been only an hour away. When he had a sudden urge to have dinner with her, he would simply call and she would be available.

Tarnower was not used to fending for himself socially. By no means did he hate to make new conquests, especially female ones, but basically he did prefer to dine and visit with people he knew quite well.

One way of looking at it would be to say that Jean Harris had spoiled Tarnower by her very availability and her close proximity. Her departure from the immediate circle of his friends could be interpreted as a blow to his social standing. As a bachelor, he needed an escort. Without Jean Harris he had no consistently available companion. He found himself invited out with no sure escort to accompany him. Not every social moment could fall only on weekends when Jean Harris was available.

The ever-resourceful Tarnower did not take a long time to find a solution. It was simplicity itself. When Jean Harris was not in town and could not accompany him on a social visit, he would invite a Jean Harris look-alike to fill the vacancy at his side.

That was, of course, Lynne Tryforos.

Whether or not Tarnower knew that he was changing pieces on a chessboard in a deliberate, even crass, manner is not important. The fact is that he effectively did exactly that.

"He didn't like to be crossed," one friend said

of Tarnower. He might have interpreted Jean Harris's departure as a deliberate move to make him feel her absence. By selecting a surrogate for her, he not only was solving his problem of a social companion, but giving one back in kind to his lover.

The "look-alike" image was deceptive. Under the surface the two women were almost complete opposites. It was here that Tarnower's vaunted ability to read character and diagnose patients deserted him completely.

Jean Harris was an intellectually brilliant, well-bred, witty, socially stimulating, attractive woman who would be considered in the top one percent of the population.

Lynne Tryforos was a lovely, sunny-dispositioned, sweet-tempered young woman who displayed an open adoration for the brilliantly learned, talented man thirty years her senior.

Once the addition of Lynne Tryforos to Tarnower's entourage became known to Jean Harris, she may well have decided to be understanding and decent about the situation. Given her personality and her upbringing, that was probably her original reaction. She probably went along with Tarnower's Machiavellian substitution—at first. After all, she did have him on weekends when her weekday stint at Madeira was over.

Aside from the other woman's looks, age, and temperament, Jean Harris could ignore her as if she never even existed. And she could possibly have done exactly that.

What Jean Harris thought about her surrogate didn't matter beans to Hi Tarnower—nor should it have mattered. He was living by his own mores. He was only doing what he had always told Jean Harris he would do—and what she had obviously known he would do.

Around the Medical Center most of Tarnower's colleagues were on to what was happening. None of them voiced an opinion about the obvious triangle.

Lynne Tryforos was well liked. "She is a lovely young lady in her early thirties who has worked with us for several years," one senior associate said. There was no mention at all about her relationship with Hi Tarnower.

Some time in 1977 Lynne Tryforos, described by another friend of Tarnower's as "a sweet innocent creature," became Tarnower's constant companion. And, as such, she became the winter girlfriend, and Jean Harris was relegated to his summer girlfriend.

The arrangement made a great deal of sense, of course, because Jean Harris got her vacation time during the warm months when school was not in session.

It may have been that Tarnower had decided on that method in order to keep the double relationship in perspective. Or it may simply have been the ultimate working out of a makeshift arrangement. But because it turned out that way—with both Lynne Tryforos and Jean Harris sharing his life—it seems evident that Tarnower did *not* want Jean Harris to drop out of the picture any more than she did.

If the summer/winter relationship seemed a perfect solution to Tarnower at the time, he had blinded himself to the facts of life. No relationship between two people ever stands still and remains static. It either advances or it retreats. Novelists know this, philosophers know this, psychologists know this, and even most lovers know this. Tarnower apparently did not.

One psychologist has put it this way:

"When Jean Harris moved to Virginia, I knew there was going to be some kind of trouble. She was mistaken to expect him not to make a substitution for her. He was no celibate. He had all the instincts of a swinging bachelor. When he decided to have his cake and eat it too—share Jean Harris with another woman—I really thought he should have had his head examined.

"The only outcome of that kind of situation would be one hell of a row. When he brought Lynne Tryforos into the picture, it was like waving a red flag in front of a bull. And I think that even a woman as cool and civilized as Jean Harris began to see red."

Tarnower himself must have sensed that things were getting out of hand a bit.

"Tarnower's love life had always been very discreet," the psychologist continued. "In Jean Harris he had chosen a very fine woman. She did not make a lot of noise about her relationship with him. In fact, from all I can gather, she kept it a deep secret. With Jean Harris as his mistress, Tarnower was assured that his professional life was safe from his personal life.

"But when Lynne Tryforos began to be a main event with Tarnower, the story was different. Jean Harris must have felt her hold on Tarnower slipping. That must have enraged her—although I don't really know the details of any confrontations she had with him.

149

"As her influence grew, the 'other woman' must have begun to sense her own strength, that she could continue to gain influence over Tarnower if she played her cards right. I see the doctor as the pawn in a game—the rope in a tug of war. Both women were pulling at him, tugging at him. Both women wanted him. He must have been absolutely mad to think he could keep the two of them happy at the same time.

"But he always had a tremendous sense of confidence about his ability to make anything he wanted work out right. It was incredible that he should not realize that people are not like figures on a charge sheet, or graphs on a cardiograph."

Before even Tarnower knew what was happening, his relationship with the two women had developed into a three-cornered war, or, as one of the doctor's neighbors in Westchester County put it:

"It was the eternal triangle, a lovers' triangle. Mrs. Harris was quite a refined lady and he baited her by taking on a young and beautiful assistant."

But there were worse surface complications than the simple fact of the triangle. Never before had Tarnower allowed his personal life to obtrude on his professional and business life. And now, suddenly, for no reason that he could discern, he was beginning to live in the middle of a volcano that seemed about to come alive and erupt at any moment.

Tarnower had always kept his relationship with Jean Harris discreet, and there had never been any hint of emotional liaison with anyone on the staff. Certainly, some of the workers at the clinic must have had dreams of relationships with their bosses—with Tarnower, as the perennial bachelor, most of all—but until Jean Harris left for Virginia, none of these "dreams" got out of hand.

Yet by no means could anyone say that the clinic became what one *New York Post* reporter called "a hotbed of jealousies among women who competed for the doctor's favor."

Tarnower did not know it, but he had made a cardinal error in strategy. There is an old saying one never makes love where one eats—that means where one makes a living. Tarnower, like thousands of bachelors before him, thought he could keep his love life and his business life separate even though he knew he was walking a thin line between two deep canyons.

Although perhaps Tarnower had infrequently—if not frequently—chosen his companions from among those who worked in and around the clinic, there was safety in numbers. With scattered individuals, there was never a concentrated relationship the way there was now with Lynne Tryforos.

Everyone knew that apart from their work at the Clinic, Tarnower and Lynne Tryforos had a personal relationship. If Tarnower was the target of affection, Lynne Tryforos suddenly became the target of disaffection.

It is unknown whether the cause was telephone calls that might have made sport of her relationship with Tarnower, or actual threats, but it is known that Lynne Tryforos suddenly had her unlisted telephone number changed to another unlisted number.

Soon after that, she changed it again!

Then, suddenly, one day, Lynne Tryforos had finished work and was ready to go home. She opened her private closet door to get out her dress. What she saw inside the closet made her give a little screech and suddenly burst into tears.

Her dress lay at the bottom of the closet floor, in shreds. Someone had ripped it and then taken a pair of scissors and cut up the pieces and thrown them in the closet.

Tarnower was appalled at what was happening. He did the best he could to smooth it over. For a time things remained calm. But once again the vendetta against Lynne Tryforos recurred. Someone had snitched her car keys, or had taken her lipstick.

Lynne Tryforos had strength of character as well as self-confidence. She continued her relationship with Tarnower, and pretended that the stormy scenes at the clinic didn't faze her at all. She was Tarnower's winter girlfriend.

During the writing of Tarnower's Scarsdale Diet book, neither woman was much concerned with the manuscript itself. Tarnower may have talked to each of them about it—but there was little participation by either of them.

He knew how much Jean Harris hated the idea of the book. He didn't want to rub it in. Once the book got into galley form and page proofs, however—things came to a head.

Even in the days when Tarnower received the first copies and showed them to the two women, he knew he was going to be in for some stormy scenes.

Each of the ladies of his life must have been annoyed at the fact that the *other* was mentioned in the book.

Jean Harris, who loathed the book and turned up her nose when she saw it anywhere, was probably absolutely stunned to see that Hi Tarnower had had the effrontery to mention the name of Lynne Tryforos on the same page on which he had thanked her!

"We are grateful to Jean Harris for her splendid assistance in the research and writing of this book . . ."

Then, only six lines later on the same page, he had written:

"We wish, especially, to thank Lynne Tryforos. . . . for [her] assistance with the diets, writing, and manuscript preparation . . . ." Even if a number of names had followed that of Lynne Tryforos, it simply made no sense for her name to appear.

What may have been even more upsetting, even nauseating to Jean Harris was that Lynne Tryforos got special mention not only on the acknowledgements page but as the name of one of the menus Tarnower had dreamed up.

On page 80, there it was:

"Spinach Delight à la Lynne," even if it was only a fancy name for creamed spinach made with yogurt.

What Jean Harris thought about those two mentions can only be imagined.

On the other hand, Lynne Tryforos was perhaps riled that Jean Harris got the big plug at the beginning of the acknowledgements.

Although there is no hard evidence of the fact, the psychological tug-of-war between the two women must have grown enormously during the summer and winter of 1979—as the Tarnower book became a best-seller and as money began to pour into the doctor's coffers.

When the winter was over, Tarnower once again returned to Jean Harris. Theoretically, he was playing the game as it should be played—without favoritism, without prejudice, and without emotion. When winter came, he was back with Lynne Tryforos. Except, that is, for one brief session with Jean Harris during her Christmas and New Year's holiday time, when Tarnower and Jean Harris went on a winter vacation together in Miami.

It was time Jean Harris could be easy and relaxed with Tarnower. She was getting more than half of the "visiting time" with him. Apparently Tarnower didn't want to cheat her out of the Christmas holiday that they had frequently spent together.

In Westchester County, Tryforos considered the ways of reaching Tarnower. She thought she knew a good one. She dialed a telephone number in New York City, and waited until the other party answered. The cost, the voice said, would be $150. And so Lynne Tryforos composed a short message on paper, and telephoned it in.

On New Year's Day, her message appeared on the front page of the *New York Times*—which Hi Tarnower, possibly along with Jean Harris, would surely be reading down in Miami.

This is what the ad, placed at the bottom of a column on the front page of the paper said:

"Happy New Year Hi T. Love Always Lynne"—Advt.

The records at the *New York Times* show that the ad was phoned in from Scarsdale—and the bill was paid by Lynne Tryforos.

What Jean Harris did or said when she saw the ad—if indeed she saw it at all—is not known.

In spite of a lot of evidence to the contrary, including the ad in the *Times*, there are those who do not believe that there ever was a serious relationship between Tarnower and Lynne Tryforos. In fact, her own sister-in-law, Mrs. Peter Tryforos of Bronxville, always insisted that there was no personal relationship with the doctor.

"As far as I know there was nothing like that," she told a *New York Post* reporter. "Lynne is a lovely woman, and she worked for several doctors at the medical center—not just Dr. Tarnower. She was an employee, and their relationship was professional. That's what I've always understood."

As for Lynne Tryforos herself, she was happy enough. Soon it would be spring and she and Tarnower would be going to Jamaica. Most of the winter, with the exception of the holidays when Jean Harris was with him, had been good for her.

10

The Thirty- Two

Tyson's Corner is a small village-like town nestled in the Virginia countryside not far from Madeira School. It has one sporting goods store, built some 53 years ago, called the Irving Sports Store. The Irving of the name no longer runs it.

One day in 1978 a woman entered the shop and said she was interested in buying a hand gun. The employee showed her different types of hand guns. Many woman prefer hand guns with calibers of about .25 or .32.

The customer finally settled on a .32 caliber Harrington & Richardson revolver with a short barrel. Most barrels are about three inches long. This was only two inches long—making the gun a short-barreled weapon.

It was necessary for the customer to fill out an application to purchase the handgun. She did so, signing her name as Jean Struven Harris. The clerk sent the application over to the Fairfax County police chief for approval.

The application was routinely reviewed by the chief and several of his men. The application had not supplied any reason for her desire to purchase the gun. Nevertheless, the request was approved and the papers returned to the store.

There would have been no reason whatsoever

to refuse Jean Harris permission to purchase a gun. Virginia was riding and shooting country, especially for the well-to-do. She looked as if she knew how to shoot and how to ride as well as anyone else in Fairfax County.

No one had the slightest suspicion that the gun would be used for anything except perhaps target practice or self-defense.

A .32 caliber revolver with a two-inch barrel is hardly a target gun, but it might be used as such.

Several weeks later Irving Sports told their customer that she could come in and pick up the revolver. She did so, paying the balance of the cost and taking the weapon with her. There is no requirement for handgun registration in Fairfax County, so there was no record of the purchase except for the approval of the chief of police on the form.

She may also have purchased ammunition at the same time. It is, in fact, quite likely that she did so.

The clerk who waited on Jean Harris has long since left the store for other employment. Although the record of the sale of the gun and the record of the sale of any possible ammunition would be noted in the store's files, these have been seized by federal agents and local police to be held for the courts.

The time of the purchase was apparently in the early months of 1978, although that is not certain. It was some months after Jean Harris had moved to Virginia to work at Madeira School.

What had happened to Jean Harris to make her decide to purchase a gun? Was she afraid for her life? Had she been threatened by some untoward incident on the campus at Madeira School? Was she fearful that the 1973 incident—the murder of the 14-year-old girl—would be repeated?

Or did her motives have nothing to do with the Madeira School at all?

Whatever the reason, she now had a .32 revolver and a box of .32 caliber bullets.

Jean Harris's life was changing, there was no question about that. Had she ever understood fully the true implications of her move from New York to Virginia or her changed position in Hi Tarnower's life?

Until she had made the break with her job in New York, Jean Harris had never been anywhere but in proximity to Tarnower—at least since after they had become intimately involved. She had no idea when she took the job that she would be creating a situation which could only end in heartbreak for her.

She mistakenly thought that her relationship with Tarnower was permanent. She knew that she would always take the bad with the good—and would reserve special days for him in her life. She failed, however, to take true measure of her man.

She thought he was strong enough to live without her nearby. He was, but he was not strong enough to resist the temptation to spend his time with other women. Jean Harris didn't think that he would quite openly choose another woman to take her place in his life. But that was exactly what he did. Tarnower's mistake was in not making a clean break with Jean Harris when he took up with Lynne Tryforos.

He would never really know his mistake.

At first Jean Harris was happy in her new job. There was always something magically exhilarating about a fresh challenge. There were certainly things that she thought should be accomplished at Madeira.

Discipline was quite lax. The students tended to be lackadaisical about their appearance, the tidiness of their rooms, and in abiding by rules and regulations of the campus.

From the beginning Jean Harris initiated a rather stern and heavy surveillance. She watched as much as she could every detail of life on campus.

Many of the students had never had "Big Sister" watching over them, but most took the new discipline in stride and obeyed the spirit as well as the letter of the new law.

The new headmistress made school history one day by banning packages of crackers in the dining room—the kind that come wrapped in cellophane with a tiny red band to tear off the wrapping. She was upset, she told the students, because the wrappers were thrown carelessly on the dining room floor.

She also banned oranges on the campus. The peels piled up everywhere. There was no need for garbage on the school grounds—the sight of it was unsightly and simply not "proper."

Later on she learned that some of the Madeira students were drinking in the taverns of the nearby Georgetown section of Washington, just across the Potomac from Madeira School. It was a place the girls liked to visit occasionally to shop and browse. Jean Harris declared the area off-limits to Madeira students.

She lectured the students once a week at a

student-body assembly. She talked so often about maintaining high moral standards, using the world "integrity" over and over, that the girls began nicknaming her "Integrity Harris."

She seemed to be instilling her high standards in the school population, and in fact during a school meeting with parents in October, 1979, she told the assembled student-body mothers that she thought many of the girls at Madeira "needed strict discipline." She got a standing ovation from the parents, and added, with rather grimly prophetic accuracy, "Aiming at a value system one can live with and be proud of takes one down a tortuous road."

Her work was tiring, even though she loved every minute of it—as she always did love any new endeavor. Then, exhausted and eager for relaxation, she would drive to her Mahopac home. On most of those occasions, she would spend part of the weekend with Hi Tarnower.

Nevertheless, within a few months after she had left for Virginia, she was hearing disquieting hints from people both she and Tarnower knew. Was there another woman? Of course, Jean Harris knew that Tarnower saw many women. But apparently this was different—this was *one* woman.

She did not want to believe it. In fact, for some time she apparently ignored the possibility. But after checking around a little, she found that it was indeed true.

Jean Harris realized she had almost deliberately brought this sorrow upon herself. She didn't know what to do. She had believed in Tarnower. She had thought he would remain true to her.

"She's a woman of strict Victorian morality," one of her friends said. "The change in Tarnower due to his involvement with another woman was shattering."

Of course, one of Jean Harris's problems was that she was indeed a strictly moral person. In developing a relationship with Tarnower, she had obviously gone against her own moral codes. She decided, however, that she could live with it.

Now, she realized she was taking too much upon herself. Her life at Madeira was totally business, and centered around the school, the students, and the staff. Jean Harris had no one to talk to on a personal level. She had no close friends. Her two sons were both grown up. One was away in the Marine Corps. The other was a banker in Yonkers, New York, engaged to be married.

It is possible that Jean Harris was lonely in her separation from the one important man in her life.

She apparently had no confidante and faced the dilemma all lonely people must face during a crisis. She was forced to ponder her troubles on her own—without the benefit of an outside ear.

She needed Tarnower more now than ever, but she had cut herself off from him by her work in Virginia. She was forced to come to this realization.

Her basic beliefs were being challenged. "She came from a background that said women marry men—they don't have affairs," one friend of hers said. "But she loved him, so she hung around."

It was easy to imagine her reasoning. She

knew that Tarnower would never marry her, because she had been through it with him time and time again.

Now that she knew there was definitely something between Tarnower and Lynne Tryforos, even though Tarnower would go out with Jean Harris and see her during the summer months and on weekends, she knew that he had another woman in his life who was as important to him as she herself used to be.

Jean Harris apparently could not bring herself to a point of decision. Perhaps she could not give Tarnower up: if he went, he must go himself. If Lynne Tryforos took him away, so be it. That may have been her attitude.

What could she do? More to the point, could she do anything?

Knowing Jean Harris's strict upbringing, her intensely moralistic philosophy of life, her aversion to violence, it is difficult to assume that she ever wanted to do Tarnower any bodily harm.

Actually, it would seem that she might prefer to harm those other women with whom he was going out every night—if it came to hurting anyone. But it is doubtful that she even thought about doing anything harmful to any of them, including Lynne Tryforos. She was simply not a violent type.

"She was getting older and she was desperate," a friend of hers told a magazine writer. "Tarnower must have been her last chance. He looked like a lizard, but he had everything she wanted—money, a prestigious career, standing. If she let him go, that meant giving up her dreams."

Well, her dreams were being shattered day by

day anyway. The fact that she was getting older was a minor point—although certainly a valid one. But why should she consider everything over and done with in her life? Why should she be desperate about her future?

She had lived a successful life already—not as successful a life as Tarnower, but successful enough. She had brought up her sons to be decent human beings. She had established herself in her profession as a figure of integrity and quality. She had fashioned moral values for the girls in the schools where she had worked, she had counseled teenagers and helped them make important decisions in their lives, she had let a bit of her aura of propriety and gentility rub off onto them.

Yet, for all of that, Jean Harris was isolated from her fellow human beings even in the heady atmosphere of the Madeira School campus. The academic life was her milieu, and even though she had become headmistress in charge of all the students, she was somehow an outsider.

"People haven't really invited me to dinner," she told a friend wistfully. "They tend to see me as an employee."

Although she had never said it, she might have felt the same way about her work at Thomas School in Connecticut.

The point was simply that without Tarnower, she had absolutely nothing in the way of a life. This consideration must certainly have entered her mind during those bleak months at Madeira as she pondered the future of her relationship with him.

Once the diet book came out, Tarnower had become instantly famous and richer. The success of the book made his name a household word. The horrible fact was, she knew, that he didn't need her any longer. If he ever had.

She once wrote in the Madeira alumnae magazine:

"If my educational philosophy has a schizophrenic ring to it, perhaps the same could be said of myself as a woman."

It was during this critical period in her life that Jean Harris may suddenly have begun to see her situation, her very self, threatened by her "rivals" for Tarnower's affections. If she would have it out with Tarnower, he apparently would quite simply remind her that he had always lived a life of freedom, choosing his companions as he wished, and that he was not about to change his ways now.

Apparently this attitude of Tarnower's goaded Jean Harris into action. It was during this period, it is suspected, that she suddenly began to make unscheduled trips to Tarnower's estate in her blue Chrysler, standing outside, watching.

The "Peeping Thomasina" syndrome, described by the *New York Post*, was "pathetic." One friend of Tarnower's—a physician closely associated with him who chooses to remain anonymous—was at the house on several occasions when this strange visitation occurred.

As he told it, Jean Harris would drive five hours up from Virginia and stand out in the wintery cold outside the Tarnower home for maybe a half an hour, gazing in fixedly at the doctor in his living room or dining room.

Then she would get back in her car and drive the five hours back to Virginia. The trips were made in January, February, and March, 1980, according to the physician who told the story.

On two occasions when Jean Harris was suspected of standing outside, Lynne Tryforos was not only the doctor's guest, but also the hostess of the evening. There never was any confrontation between the two women, the source of information said.

"We called her the 'unwelcome woman who came to dinner,' " said Tarnower's associate. "She just stood there looking as distraught and forlorn as a person could look. She didn't say anything, and she never seemed to move. She was like some kind of an apparition.

"She didn't look at anybody but Hi, and after awhile, she was gone," he recalled. "It was spooky."

According to the *Post*, Jean Harris appeared at the house during three dinner parties, and at other times when Tarnower was alone.

Not only did several of Tarnower's other colleagues confirm this strange story, but so did a friend of Lynne Tryforos's.

"It was pathetic," said an employee of Tarnower's clinic, who claims she spotted Jean Harris the first night she appeared at one of the doctor's legendary dinner parties.

"Hi just shook his head," she related, "and we all went back to our meal and our conversation and tried to pretend that nothing upsetting had just happened. Apparently he'd been trying to let Jean down easily for years."

Early in 1980, Jean Harris's eldest son David was married. Upon graduation from college, he had taken a job as a banker in Yonkers, New York. When his mother lived in New York and worked in Connecticut and New York, he saw her frequently.

But when she moved to Virginia, he did not see her as much. Nevertheless, when he was married in February, 1980, Hi Tarnower gave him a wedding dinner at his home.

Long before, of course, Jean Harris had been faced with the "empty nest" syndrome so popular with the magazine writers. Her other son James had joined the Marine Corps and was now a lieutenant. They had both left home some years before and it was one reason that Jean Harris felt the need for the companionship of Tarnower.

David's marriage was simply one more inexorable step in her life, and it more or less helped intensify her loneliness.

Naturally, because she was a most self-contained woman who had never made unjust demands on the members of her family, Jean Harris did not discuss her personal situation with her sons or her daughter-in-law at any time during those long years either.

It was not the proper thing for Jean Harris to do—even now that America seemed to have a casual lifestyle. Certainly both sons knew Tarnower and what he was to their mother.

Jean Harris was beginning to feel that her entire world was crumbling beneath her feet. She must have been sure now that Tarnower was seeing more of Lynne Tryforos than ever before. She had read his acknowledgement to her in his book; he had given one of his recipes her name!

During her vacation in Miami with Tarnower, she had probably seen the advertisement on the front page of the New York Times. It can be imagined with what contempt and disdain she viewed its lack of taste!

Shortly after her son David's marriage, Jean Harris learned that Tarnower had gone on a vacation with Lynne Tryforos to Jamaica. Of course, it *was* school time, and Jean Harris should not have been surprised.

Right on top of that blow—we must assume it *was* a blow to Jean Harris—there occurred a situation at Madeira School that was extremely upsetting.

Apparently administration officials somehow got wind of marijuana smoking that was going on in one or several of the school's dormitory rooms, and it was Jean Harris—again, it has to be assumed—who gathered together several of her staff and conducted an extensive search through the dormitory rooms. Sure enough, pot and marijuana smoking paraphernalia were located and confiscated.

The occupants of the rooms where the marijuana was discovered were immediately confronted with the evidence and told that they were guilty of breaking the school's rules.

But these were no ordinary students. A group of four was involved. Three of the four were members of the school's judiciary committee! And all four of the girls were among the most popular and highly-thought-of on campus.

There was, according to reports, a very emotional confrontation between Jean Harris and the four transgressors. The girls were told that there was only one possible action that could be taken. They would have to leave the school because they had broken the rules.

There were apparently tears and highly emotional appeals, but Jean Harris did not give in. She may have told the students that she would not change her decision for any reason. If she did, it would have been in character.

She may have reminded them that since they had flown in the face of convention—and the law—they would have to suffer the consequences.

Shortly after the confrontation, Jean Harris is said to have convened a board of school officials and taken a vote on the expulsion of the students. The vote to expell carried.

Once a week the headmistress addressed the school's entire student body on public affairs. At the meeting on Friday, March 7, the last day of school before three weeks of spring vacation, she announced the expulsion of the four students and the rationale for the punishment.

Although it was not a usual occurrence, several students—not those involved in the incident—voiced the opinion that they disagreed with the dormitory search and the expulsion procedures.

It can be assumed that Jean Harris was shocked at the sudden and unexpected show of strength against her and her regime. She had always suspected *some* resentment against the strictures of discipline she had instituted, but it had never come out in the open like this before—not in front of the entire student body.

Memories of the banning of oranges, and crackers, and the banning of Georgetown were apparently quite vivid in the minds of some of the students.

Jean Harris stood her ground. The expulsion of the four students was a fait accompli. The meeting apparently ended in some disagreement and with a sense of muted controversy stirring, but Jean Harris did not seem unduly disturbed.

One of the school's board of directors said later: "Jean Harris showed no signs of stress on Friday night."

The headmistress was telling everyone that she would be staying on the campus for the entire vacation period, and would have several meetings on Monday. Monday night she had a dinner date with her friends John and Kiku Haines in Washington.

Not all the students went home on Friday night. Some had things to do, and some had friends they wanted to hang out with. Some of them came in to talk to Jean Harris and wish her a happy vacation. Perhaps some of them wanted to sympathize with her over the fact that she had been forced to expel four of their classmates.

Some of them noticed that the usually neat little house was in a disheveled condition. It was not at all like Jean Harris—any more than it was like her to present a disheveled appearance at any time.

Jean Harris was beginning to show the effects of the marijuana incident. It seemed to be taking its toll on her as much as on the students. This was an unexpected development. Jean Harris did not usually allow her feelings to show.

Many of them must have wondered why the incident should be leaving its marks on her. Most of them were puzzled.

If they had been privy to her private life with Hi Tarnower, they might have been able to piece together the parts of the puzzle. But none of the students knew about her double life. None knew

169

about her rapidly escalating crisis with Tarnower in her "other life."

At Madeira she was the image of strict conformity, strong convictions, and an acceptance of law and order. As the symbol of probity, she was the person on campus who was authorized to exact punishment for trespasses. In other words, she was the judge, the jury, and the enforcer in addition. But in her private life, it was not as easy to bring in a sound judgment, or enforce that judgment. She was in the awkward position of acting as a professional moral and social arbiter while, in her own life, the issues were not so clear.

Quite probably, it was at this point that she began a considerable reevaluation. Her sons were grown up and had left home. The most important man in her life was living miles and hours away and other women were filling his time and her space. Only her professional life was stable. After all, she was proving herself capable of doing her job.

It was at this point we can suppose that she may have contemplated putting an end to the dreary conflict. No one can say that she decided to do away with herself. Nor, perhaps, did she have this idea in mind at all. But somehow, it must have been driven home to her that she could not make Tarnower change his mind and marry her, that she could not make Tarnower's other woman leave him, that she could not resolve all the difficulties she found in her own life.

Her life, she might well have reasoned, was as good as over. Tarnower had ruined what little of the good life she had. He was responsible for this change—running around with all those women.

What mortified her, quite possibly, was that Tarnower did not even know what he was doing to her! That was the "most unkindest cut of all."

Somehow Jean Harris got through that weekend before the spring vacation. She did appear upset, uncomfortable, and quite beside herself even to her colleagues, but none of them questioned her about it.

They presumed that her emotional state had something to do with the marijuana bust and the subsequent dismissals. But they didn't know the whole story.

On Monday morning she had a meeting at nine o'clock. In spite of the fact that she was still showing some signs of unrest over the expulsions, she appeared composed and quite normal.

But when she got back to "The Hill" she apparently wrote a series of notes to people on campus, to relatives, and a letter to Hi Tarnower. Either she began to compose the notes and letter at that time, or she continued to do what she might have begun earlier. No one knows when the eight notes and the letter were started.

Her exact state of mind at the time is also unknown. It is unknown because the notes and the letter—a rambling ten-page effusion addressed to Hi Tarnower—are now in the hands of the authorities. The eight notes belong to the prosecution; the registered letter belongs to the defense.

The registered letter contains, it is said, "a rundown of what [Tarnower's] behavior had done to her." At times rambling, loving, apologetic, and filled with hurt, it becomes confused at the end and is not even signed, according to those who have seen it.

In fact, when Jean Harris had finished writing the letter, she simply crammed the pages into the envelope in random order and sealed it shut.

As for the notes, some are said to ask friends to provide for disposal of her body and possessions. It is said that these notes manifest her own bleak mental state, her knowledge that her own death was very near, although the word "suicide" was apparently never used.

As for the long epistle she wrote to Tarnower, it was posted as a registered letter at the campus post office, where she signed a receipt for it. The eight notes were not posted to anyone, but remained in a confused heap on her desk at home in "The Hill."

It is not known at what time of the day she placed a telephone call to Westchester County, but she did do so sometime on Monday, presumably after she had posted the registered letter.

Whether or not she talked to Tarnower in Scarsdale is not known, either. But what is known is that after the posting of the letter and the telephone call—in whatever order they occurred—she was an entirely different person.

She had promised to attend a three-o'clock meeting that afternoon. She did not show up. She did not call to excuse herself. She gave no explanation whatsoever for missing the meeting. She saw no one.

Later on, that evening, she was supposed to attend the home of her friends, the Haineses, in

Washington. She did not call to excuse herself or to offer any explanation as to why she would not come to dinner.

"When she didn't show up for my dinner," Kiku Haines explained, "my first instinct was that something had come up at the School."

However, Haines did not try to get in touch with her. If she had, she would quite probably not have reached her at "The Hill."

It is a five-hour drive from the Madeira School campus to Tarnower's residence in Purchase. Jean Harris must have left Virginia sometime around five or six o'clock in the evening.

The next thing anyone knew about her was her appearance at the Tarnower estate in Westchester, soaking wet from the rainstorm that assaulted the East Coast.

Jean Harris was distraught. She bore a visible bruise on her mouth, and she had a recently-fired, blood-stained revolver in a box in the glove compartment of her car.

11

The Arraignment

Herman Tarnower was dead.

He had died of bullet wounds that he had received in his bedroom. A gun had been found by the police that might have been the weapon that fired the bullets.

Tarnower had been hit four times: in the hand, in the arm, in the shoulder, and in the chest.

The police were holding a suspect in the slaying.

In fact, she had at the scene of the crime reportedly said that she thought she had killed Hi Tarnower.

Even before Tarnower had died and shortly after the suspect had turned over the gun she had bought in Tyson's Corners, the police had taken her to the Harrison Police Station.

There they interrogated her.

During the interrogation they elicited the following statements from Jean Harris.

Asked about her relationship with Tarnower, she said a number of different things.

"I have been through so much hell with him," she said.

What kind of hell?

"He slept with every woman he could."

How did she feel about him?

"I loved him very much." But, she added after a moment: "I had it."

What happened on the night Tarnower was shot?

Jean Harris said that she had driven up to Tarnower's home from Madeira School in Virginia.

Did she bring the .32 caliber revolver found in her glove compartment with her?

"Yes," she said.

Was it loaded?

"Yes."

Had she come with the intention of killing Tarnower?

"No," she said. She had come to his home to ask him to kill her. "I wanted to die. Why should he die?"

What happened when she got to the house?

She entered the house and found him in the bedroom. A quarrel started.

What was the quarrel about?

She said that she asked the doctor to kill her because she wanted to die. He refused to do so.

How did Tarnower react?

At one point, she recalled, he said, "You are crazy. Get out of here!"

Did that end the quarrel?

No, she told them. They began to fight once again. Somehow, in the struggle she received a blow in the mouth that gave her a bruised lip, and perhaps a slap in the eye. "He hit me," she said. "He hit me a lot."

Who had the gun? Who shot it?

"I remember holding the gun and I shot him in the hand," she said.

Then later on, when she was again asked if she had the gun all the time, she said, "I don't know who had control of the gun." After a moment, she said, "I threw the gun in the bathtub."

But sometime before that, she had told the police that the gun was in her car. And that was where they had recovered it.

At one point in the interrogation, Jean Harris moaned wearily and cried out, "Why didn't you kill me, Hi?"

At another time, she observed that it was "ironic that Dr. Tarnower was dying" and that she was living.

Why?

Because it was she who wanted to die and he who wanted to live.

She was asked again and again if she really had come up to Purchase to have Tarnower kill her.

"Yes," she said. "I had no intention of going back to Virginia alive."

She showed the police a list of names.

"These are names of close relatives to be notified after my wishes were completed." She apparently meant that the people on the list were to be notified of her death after she had been killed by Tarnower.

Did she have any more notes?

At that point she remembered that she had left a number of notes back at Madeira School. She said they were in her home. In addition to those notes, she had written a long letter to Tarnower.

Where was the letter?

She said she had posted it Registered Mail to Dr. Herman Tarnower.

At one point during her interrogation, she suddenly looked up at the police who were surrounding her and snapped at them, "Who did he have over to dinner?"

When she was told that Tarnower's sister was there, and his niece, Jean Harris said nothing. Then they said that Lynne Tryforos was there, too. Jean Harris nodded grimly, as if she had thought it might be that way.

During the interrogation she was examined by a police matron. According to the reports, she had sustained a bruise on the mouth, a slight discoloration of the eye, and a long black and blue bruise that extended from her inner elbow seven inches up, almost to her armpit.

While the interrogation of Jean Harris was under way, the technical investigation of the crime continued. That is, the medical team examined the dead body, the photographic team took pictures at the site of the murder, and the fingerprint team went over the physical evidence on the second floor of the Purchase Street residence.

This was to establish the physical facts of the *corpus delicti*—the term so happily favored by crime writers who do not really know that it means the "fact or facts necessary to the commission of a crime" rather than the "corpse of the victim" (*corpus* means "body" rather than "corpse").

(Webster says: "*Corpus delicti*. The substantial and fundamental fact or facts necessary to the commission of a crime, as in murder the actual death of the person alleged to have been murdered, and as a result of criminal agency—often erroneously to designate the physical

177

body of the victim of a murder.'')

Deputy Medical Examiner Dr. Louis Roh of Westchester County was in charge of the examination of Tarnower's body. Preliminary investigation showed him that Tarnower had been shot in four places: the hand, the arm, the shoulder, and the chest.

But only three bullets were removed from the body. These were set aside for ballistics tests to determine whether they had been fired from the Harrington & Richardson revolver turned over to the police by Jean Harris.

Three of the rounds that had struck Tarnower had entered on the right side of his body in the front. The fourth round, however, had entered his body from the back. Roh postulated that the victim had turned around, apparently trying to get away from the bullets coming at him, or, perhaps, he had stumbled back from the body blows and had turned around in falling to the floor.

The Harrington & Richardson revolver was a six-shot weapon. There was one bullet left in the chamber. According to the police laboratory, the gun had been fired at least five times. The problem was—where were the two missing bullets?

The bullets which had made three of the entry holes in the body had been recovered from inside the body. The fourth bullet had apparently gone through the body. The fifth bullet must have missed the body entirely.

The detective detail working on the Tarnower bedroom finally found the fourth bullet—the one that had supposedly passed through Tarnower's hand. It had lodged in a wooden bookcase near the twin beds.

When the detectives measured the angle of the bullet as it struck, it became obvious that the fourth bullet had not been fired in the same direction as the other slugs, but that it may have been fired from the same point.

The fifth bullet was never found during the preliminary investigation. Speculation was that it may have passed through a bedroom window. However, it was not immediately ascertained why a window in the bedroom should have been wide open with a fierce rainstorm whipping across the estate's grounds outside.

Now a new character appeared in the Tarnower/Harris/Tryforos story. His name was Joel M. Aurnou. His appearance would not usually have been a part of an Agatha Christie country-mansion mystery novel. Aurnou was a lawyer who specialized in criminal defense.

But his presence in the present story was necessary because charges were about to be filed against Jean Harris. The Agatha Christie story was slowly turning into an Erle Stanley Gardiner mystery novel, featuring Perry Mason.

How Aurnou was approached to rush to the defense of Jean Harris is not known, but before the dust had settled, he was there with his client making sure the interrogation went right.

Aurnou was a man who might have just stepped out of the pages of a courtroom novel. A flamboyant, articulate, aggressive and shrewd attorney, Aurnou was usually seen either chewing the nibs of his horn-rimmed glasses, or mouthing a smouldering cigar.

A feisty, rough-tough courtroom lawyer, he had made his name during three earlier highly publicized trials in Westchester County. One was the Caramoor art theft; another a New Rochelle kidnapping; and the third a Mount Vernon police probe.

In 1972, art work valued at about $500,000 was stolen from the Caramoor Center for Music and Art in Katonah, a town in the northern section of Westchester. Aurnou and Leon Greenspan, who was his law partner at the time—the two have gone their separate ways since—were contacted by the thieves.

Aurnou went to the District Attorney of Westchester County with a proposition. If the D.A. would not prosecute the thieves, the two attorneys would arrange for the art to be returned.

The D.A. blew his top. Aurnou had his nerve, and so did the thieves—etc. However, a deal was apparently arranged.

The following month the art was returned in exchange for promises that the thieves would be given immunity from prosecution. The art works were handed over in the parking lot at the Jewish Community Center in White Plains.

Six months later, the D.A. suddenly persuaded the grand jury to indict the Caramoor thieves for a burglary that they had committed *prior* to the art theft.

Now Aurnou was fit to be tied. He claimed that the D.A. had doublecrossed both him and his clients. He said the alleged "immunity" promise that had been arranged extended to all prior crimes. He also maintained that the case had been investigated and brought to a conclusion by the use of wiretaps—which, of course, were illegal.

The appeals court ruled finally in favor of Aurnou's clients. The indictments were dismissed. But in spite of the victory, Aurnou was upset. Rumors began to surface that Aurnou was actually a co-conspirator in the Caramoor case.

That didn't sit well with him at all—but his day was coming.

Shortly after the Caramoor caper, indictments were announced against two men who were accused of running a prostitution ring in New Rochelle. Aurnou claimed the D.A.—or someone in his office—had committed a misdemeanor by allegedly deliberately leaking the details of the indictments to the press before they were unsealed in court.

The give-and-take between Aurnou and the Westchester County District Attorney was beginning to boil up into a rough-and-tumble, old-fashioned feud.

If Aurnou was Perry Mason, the D.A. was definitely Ham Burger.

In this particular incarnation, the District Attorney was a prosecutor named Carl A. Vergari. The conflict that had been simmering between Aurnou and Vergari for so long a time was ready for a full eruption. That finally occurred in 1974.

And the cockpit was the political arena, not the courts. Democrat Joel M. Aurnou took it upon himself to try to unseat Republican Carl A. Vergari and win his post. There was a lot of name-calling in the campaign, a lot of heavy press for both candidates, and a lot of really vicious in-fighting.

In one instance, Aurnou called Vergari a

"Piper Cub pilot trying to fly a 747." He also accused his opponent of "unparalleled delay" in prosecuting cases. He cited him for failing to launch a speedy investigation of corruption in the Mount Vernon police department.

The details of the corruption came from a convicted gambler who was kidnapped in New Rochelle by one of Aurnou's clients. The gambler told Aurnou that he had regularly paid "hush" money to a number of policemen.

In addition to his charges that Vergari had failed to investigate this corruption, Aurnou said that Vergari had prior knowledge of a planned escape of two inmates at the county penitentiary in 1973. And he criticized him for failing to prosecute as many cases as he should in Westchester.

"Hasn't he fooled you long enough?" said a headline on the campaign literature that Aurnou handed out, showing a picture of Vergari.

Vergari didn't let Aurnou get away with any of this without a fight. He said that Aurnou had "completely and deliberately distorted" his court record. He said Aurnou's statements reflected a "total lack of criminal justice experience" and described Aurnou as "the man who as defense counsel in Westchester stands up and tells the judges the same boring and tiresome stories that his defendant who has committed a crime is really a nice boy."

Vergari said that Aurnou's charges were "a reckless political smear from a desperate candidate whose campaign hasn't come off the ground."

The public apparently agreed with Vergari. He won reelection in November, 1974.

However, in the spring of 1977, Aurnou was suddenly appointed by Governor Hugh Carey to the County Court bench to fill a vacancy.

But if he wanted to keep the job, he would have to win an election in November. That meant that he would need to project an image of a tough judge, not that of a flamboyant defense attorney who might be good at getting "guilty" people off the hook.

A defendant named Patricia Silberstein was convicted of manslaughter in the death of a man named Anthony Wojcik who was killed at the Mount Vernon incinerator. She was sentenced in Aurnou's court. Aurnou set a minimum prison term of seven years and a maximum of 22 years seven months and 22 days for her. He based those odd figures on the date she had killed the victim.

Courthouse buffs were astounded at Aurnou's action. He was roundly criticized for making a "cheap attempt" to grab publicity with his get-tough sentencing. Eventually the Appellate Division of the State Supreme Court reduced the sentence to three to fifteen years rather than the seven to twenty-two Aurnou had specified.

"They've had a war going for quite some time," said one long-term courthouse observer. "It's personal, there's no question about it. It goes beyond just a district attorney and a defense attorney because of the two people involved. Joel gets wound up easily and tends to go off the deep end before he realized he's at that point. And Vergari, well, Vergari is just very impressed with Vergari."

"It's definitely a personality conflict," said

Leon Greenspan, Aurnou's previous law partner. "Vergari has a personal dislike for Joel that transcends everything."

Aurnou, for his part, had always denied that his conflicts with Vergari ever had any personal overtones. "No way. We're both professionals. It doesn't go beyond that to personalities."

Nevertheless, the feud was still simmering.

And here was Aurnou, getting ready to defend Jean Harris in one of the most sensational cases ever to hit Westchester County.

Item: the fatal shooting of a millionaire author/physician.

Item: the arrest of his socialite former girlfriend.

Item: the possibility of romantic jealousy as a motive.

How Aurnou got into the Jean Harris/Hi Tarnower case, or who summoned him, or what happened that eventually caused Joel Aurnou to be Jean Harris's counselor, is not known. But he got there at some time during the questioning that took up most of the long night of March 10-11.

And apparently, he was with her much of Tuesday, March 11. It was either during the night or during that day that Aurnou learned about the long letter that Jean Harris had sent to Hi Tarnower.

In fact, Jean Harris is said to have pleaded with the police when they were questioning her at the Harrison Police Station to return to her a registered letter she had mailed to Tarnower on Monday.

When Jean Harris told her counselor about the letter, he realized it might be an important piece of evidence, especially if it contained the information that she said it did.

If it contained, in effect, an account of her feelings toward Tarnower and of her confusion as to what she should do about their relationship, it might certainly be evidence of her state of mind. Aurnou knew that if he could show that she was indeed "disturbed," he might be able to prove that she did not know what she was doing when she found herself with Tarnower in his bedroom that night.

There is no first-degree murder in New York State—except for that involving an officer of the law as the victim. The highest degree of murder for a crime involving civilians is second-degree murder. A lesser charge is manslaughter, both first-degree and second-degree.

To prove "murder" of any kind, the prosecution must deomonstrate "intent to kill." Aurnou was counting on the fact that a "disturbed" mind cannot be proved to have "intent." In the case of Jean Harris the one key word for her defense was "intent."

First-degree manslaughter is a charge referring to a case in which someone kills a victim with the intention of injuring him seriously, or kills a victim while suffering from an extreme emotional disturbance.

Second-degree manslaughter is a charge referring to a case in which someone kills a victim through recklessness—as in an automobile accident when one driver is exceeding the speed limit or the limits of reasonably responsible driving.

To Aurnou, the two key words were "intent" and "disturbance." If Jean Harris never had the intention of killing Tarnower, murder could not be proved. If she was suffering from an extreme emotional "disturbance," she might be charged with only first-degree manslaughter, rather than murder.

It was up to Aurnou to prove that Jean Harris was "disturbed" enough not to know her own mind at the time of the Tarnower shooting. If he could prove that, he could quite probably get the charge reduced to manslaughter—and might eventually be able to get her off completely by showing how upset she was.

The most important thing right away was to get the letter she had written to Tarnower. First of all, he had to determine what was in it. If Jean Harris was lying about what the letter contained, and if indeed it did say that she was going to drive up to Westchester to kill Tarnower, he would have to know about it immediately in order to prepare a different type of case.

If she was telling the truth, which was highly likely, and if the letter *did* contain her stated purpose in driving up to Westchester—in effect, to get Tarnower to kill her—then he would be able to base his case on the letter itself, along with other evidence about her relationship with Tarnower.

Whether or not Jean Harris discussed Lynne Tryforos with Aurnou—and to what extent if she did—is not known, but it is quite probable that she did. Aurnou knew about the "other woman" by the time he met with the press on Tuesday. In a legal sense, the evidence that there was a third party in the relationship between Jean Harris and Hi Tarnower was a plus for the prosecution, not the defense.

All the prosecutor had to prove was that Jean

Harris was jealous of Lynne Tryforos and resented Tarnower's attention to her to establish a motive for the killing of Tarnower. It would be expedient for Aurnou to do all he could to disprove any obvious hints of jealousy in Jean Harris directed against Lynne Tryforos.

Aurnou had a lot going for him already. Officer O'Sullivan had written about four pages of notes at the Tarnower house. It was he who said that Jean Harris "had driven up from Virginia with the intention of having Dr. Tarnower kill her."

And he had also reported: "She said she had left notes in her Virginia home indicating what she intended to do in New York. She stated that she'd had no intention of going back to Virginia alive."

There it was. The intention, according to her statement in the policeman's notes, was not to kill Tarnower, but to have him kill her. But Aurnou wanted more proof of that than simply the hearsay evidence of the interrogating officer.

Perhaps in the letter she said she had written to Tarnower she might have put down in black and white that she intended to have him kill her.

By now a number of important legal events had occurred. Most important was the fact that Jean Harris was arraigned in Harrison Town Court on Tuesday afternoon. A court hearing was scheduled for Thursday afternoon, March 13, to determine whether or not there was enough evidence to turn the case over to a Westchester grand jury.

During the arraignment, Aurnou said, "I've learned nothing so far that would support a charge of intentional homicide. [The police] have nothing more than an impression from [Jean Harris] who is in shock.''

The court session was very short—only about two minutes—and after it was over Jean Harris was led off again. She spent Tuesday night in the women's section of the County Jail in Valhalla.

During the time Jean Harris was arraigned and as she was being taken to the Valhalla jail, the ballistics tests were being administered on the handgun she had turned over to the police.

In the ballistics laboratory, .32 caliber bullets were loaded into the .32 caliber Harrington & Richardson revolver, and the weapon was fired into a large box-like device padded with cotton batting used to slow down slugs and stop them without injury.

Retrieved from the cotton inside the device, the slugs were compared under microscope with the slugs that Roh had removed from Tarnower's body. The evidence clearly showed that the slugs fired from the .32 caliber Harrington & Richardson weapon had been fired from the same weapon which had shot the slugs that entered Tarnower's body.

That meant, without question, that the gun taken from the box in Jean Harris's glove compartment was the gun that had fired the shots that killed Tarnower.

Meanwhile the police laboratory was busy testing a sample of the blood that had dried on the surface of the revolver. It was ascertained to be type B blood—a type rarer than both types O and A.

Dr. Herman Tarnower's blood type was B.

Jean Harris had not sustained any wounds that had led to bleeding during the scuffle in the bedroom.

This meant that the blood on the handgun was probably Tarnower's.

Aurnou had already requested that his client be allowed her freedom on bail; a bail hearing was set for the following day, Wednesday, March 12.

By now, Aurnou's old courtroom adversary, District Attorney Carl Vergari, was in on the action. He had seen the ballistics reports that showed the Jean Harris gun to be the one that killed Tarnower.

His decision was that there was definitely enough to charge the suspect with second-degree murder. He felt that the county had enough evidence to sustain the charge. But he wanted more time to develop evidence.

In Westchester County, local courts are not allowed to set bail in cases of murder. Such requests—like Aurnou's—must be made in county court.

At the bail hearing in White Plains, Westchester County court Judge John C. Couzens heard the bail case on Wednesday.

Deputy Westchester Medical Examiner Dr. Louis Roh testified first that Tarnower had been shot in the hand, the arm, the shoulder, and the chest, and that three bullets had been removed from his body.

Westchester Police Commissioner Thomas A. Delaney then testified: "Ballistics tests positively identified the gun as the one used in the killing." He explained that it had been emptied of five bullets, of which three had been recovered from the victim's body.

Joel Aurnou's argument for bail was

189

postulated mainly on the point that Jean Harris should be released on bail in order to get "immediate medical attention." He pointed out that she had three bruises, two on her face and one on her arm.

He said that he was trying to arrange for consultation with a psychiatrist, and that it was not in her best interest to be locked up in jail. Besides that, she was "a very fine lady of the kind you don't see anymore, but who is in a state of emotional shock." He said that she had been a "teacher all her life." Her reputation was "absolutely flawless," he said.

Responding to those pleas, Assistant District Attorney Joseph Rackaky said that it was "premature to make judgments" about the nature of the shooting. He pointed out that Jean Harris did attempt to leave the scene of the shooting before the police arrived there.

"The weapon in question was brought to the scene by this defendant. She took it out of a box in her car."

The report of the Harrison police was that Jean Harris was driving away from the house when a police car arrived. She turned around and went back to the house, allegedly telling the officers, "There's been a shooting."

And, Rackaky said, "She shot him four times. I think that negates any question of self-defense. True, she had one bruised lip, but that is no comparison to being shot to death."

Rackaky recommended that Jean Harris be held without bail.

Aurnou's response to the implication that Jean Harris was "fleeing the scene of the crime" was that she had left the house to find a telephone because the phone in Dr. Tarnower's bedroom did not work. Then, when the police arrived, Aurnou said, she "returned entirely of her own volition."

And, Aurnou said, "There is nothing I've heard or seen to indicate that this was an intentional killing."

Aurnou also mentioned the "condition of the gun when it was found," referring to police reports that the gun was in two parts—"broken down"—when it was taken out of its box in the glove compartment of Jean Harris's car.

He then pointed out that Jean Harris had a substantial personal reputation as well as "roots in the community." This particular factor is generally an essential criterion for the posting of bail.

The defense attorney said that the defendant had had offers of two temporary places of residence locally—the home of her 29-year-old son, David, a banker who lived in Yonkers, and the home of a lawyer whom Aurnou did not identify.

The main factors in a bail hearing are the defendant's community ties and the past criminal record. The law also instructs judges to study the defendant's character and reputation, along with the weight of the evidence against the defendant, and the possible sentence.

The basic reason for the granting of bail is to assure a defendant's appearance in court at a later date rather than to become an instrument for detention of a person before trial.

Aurnou reminded Judge Couzens that he had released other defendants on $40,000 bail under similar conditions in the past.

When the judge asked Aurnou if Jean Harris could live within the confines of Westchester county pending further legal action, Aurnou assured him that she could.

When the arguments were through, Judge Couzens made his decision. He agreed with Aurnou. "This is a schoolteacher," he told Rackaky. But he told Aurnou that Jean Harris would be required to stay within the boundaries of Westchester County to await whatever resolution there might be to the charges against her.

A preliminary hearing had been scheduled as noted for Thursday, March 13, to determine if there was sufficient evidence to warrant a study of the case by the grand jury. Whatever the grand jury decided—and what charges would be levied against her—would determine the fate of her case in the courts.

The grand jury could take two courses: it could dismiss the case for lack of evidence, or for any other reason; or it could decide to try the case under whatever charges it thought proper.

She could be charged with second-degree murder, that is, murder with intent; first-degree manslaughter, or second-degree manslaughter.

At the preliminary hearing on Thursday Jean Harris would be required to be present. Bail was granted, in the sum of $40,000.

The next few hours were spent raising bail. "Jean Harris has a home in Mahopac," Aurnou said, "but there is not enough equity for the amount we need."

Present at the court were the members of Jean Harris's immediate family. Her son James Harris, a lieutenant in the U.S. Marines, had flown up from Marine Camp in the South to be with her. Her son David had come over immediately and had arranged to stay with her once she was free again.

Her brother Captain Robert Struven of the U.S. Navy had flown in from San Diego where he was stationed. Jean Harris's sisters Mary Margaret Lynch of Shaker Heights, Ohio, and Virginia McLaughlin of Cleveland, Ohio, were also present.

The only persons close to her who were not there were her mother and father, who were in Florida. Her former husband, James Harris, had died in 1977.

It was Captain Struven who put up two $10,000 certificates of deposit, and Mary Lynch who put up a $20,000 certificate of deposit.

In order to post bail, Jean Harris appeared in court briefly after bail was set to swear to the truth of the statements she had been required to make in the bond application.

As the hearing concluded, dozens of media people—newspaper reporters, television and radio interviewers, and camera and sound crews—milled about in the front of Harrison Town Court.

Aurnou, with all the instincts of a magician, grabbed Jean Harris quickly by the arm and the two slipped unobtrusively out the back door of the courthouse.

Loud cries of anguish went up from the press when its members learned they had been hoodwinked by Aurnou. But it was too late to catch Jean Harris. They had to be satisfied photographing Jean Harris's family. But they vowed not to be taken in next time by Aurnou's tricky back-door departure tactics.

12

The Adversaries

Joel Aurnou's work was cut out for him. By the
time the arraignment and the bail hearing were
over on Wednesday, he knew exactly in what
direction he must go. Once out of court, he
closeted himself with his law partner, John
Kelligrew, to work out their next moves.

Of crucial interest to Aurnou and to his client
Jean Harris was the letter she had written to Tarnower and had posted by registered mail from
the post office on the campus at Madeira
School. Aurnou wanted the letter. He needed it
for the case. He determined to get it at all costs.
It had been addressed, according to Jean Harris,
to Tarnower at the Scarsdale Medical Center,
and not to him at his home.

Aurnou guessed that it would probably be
delivered sometime Wednesday at the Scarsdale
post office. It was a point of law that the sender
of any letter can always reclaim it before its
delivery to the recipient. Once the letter is
delivered, the sender no longer has any claim on
it.

In this case, there could be no quarrel between
the sender and recipient, because there was only
one who wanted it and she was the only one alive
who could have it. The point was for Aurnou to

claim the letter in the name of Jean Harris.

A quick and discreet query at the post office assured Aurnou and Kelligrew that the letter had indeed already been requested by members of the District Attorney's office.

Following the letter of the law, the postmaster would turn the letter over to the District Attorney's office only if the D.A. managed to get a court order to that effect. He had told the D.A.'s people that. As yet, the letter had not been delivered to the post office, nor had the District Attorney procured the court order to intercept it.

Quickly Aurnou and Kelligrew prepared the proper papers to secure the letter from the postal authorities. The paperwork required included three key documents:

● One was a form called "Sender's Application for Recall to Mail." That was duly filled out by Aurnou and Kelligrew and signed by Jean Harris. She gave as a reason for wanting to recall the letter that the addressee was deceased.

● The second form essential to securing the letter was the receipt for the registered letter Jean Harris had filled out when she posted the envelope on the Madeira campus on Monday.

● The third form was a notarized affidavit authorizing John Kelligrew to act on her behalf in picking up the letter in question.

Meanwhile, Samuel Morrison, the Postmaster at the Scarsdale Post Office, was busy doing his legal homework. The District Attorney's office had already alerted him to the fact that Tarnower was dead. The morning papers were heralding that fact to everyone else in the world.

Morrison consulted with postal lawyers to

find out what to do about the letter when it did come. And Morrison got his answer. He had been absolutely correct in telling the District Attorney's office that it would take a federal court order to get the letter.

When Kelligrew arrived at the post office and spoke with Morrison, Morrison checked out the forms, compared them with the check list he had been given by postal lawyers, and told Kelligrew that as soon as the letter came, it would be his.

About 5 p.m. on Wednesday a bulky yellowish manilla-type #10 envelope—9 1/2 by 4 inches in size—came to the Scarsdale Post Office. It was addressed to Dr. Herman Tarnower at his office in the Scarsdale Medical Center, 259 Heathcote Road. The word "Personal" was marked in heavy letters on the front of the envelope.

In the upper left-hand corner, the envelope bore the return address of the Office of Headmistress of Madeira School in Virginia. Morrison took the forms from Kelligrew and Kelligrew took the envelope.

"The letter was turned over because that is the normal process," Morrison later told members of the press. "A customer has the right to recall any mail before it is delivered. You just need the right paperwork."

Finally, at about 1:15 p.m. on Thursday—almost a day after Kelligrew had secured the letter with the three forms of recall— Detective Lieutenant Alfred Della Rocco of the Harrison Town Police arrived at the post office. He now had the Federal court order for the letter in question.

And he learned that the letter had been picked

up the day before by "someone" from Aurnou's office.

"We were scooped," a member of the D.A.'s office ruefully admitted.

In addition to that, Della Rocco learned that the papers he had were the wrong ones, anyway.

There is no record of what District Attorney Carl Vergari said or did when he learned of this somewhat revolting turn of events.

But whatever it was, there was not the slightest doubt about it. The Vergari/Aurnou feud was on again—and this time it was blazing on the top burner.

Nevertheless, reaction was immediate. Vergari wasted not a minute before putting the wheels in motion to issue a subpoena to both Aurnou and Kelligrew to appear on Friday before the grand jury investigating the Tarnower killing—*with the letter in question.*

Aurnou and Kelligrew received the subpoena papers with eloquent shrugs. "I'm unclear how this fits into the attorney-client relationship," Aurnou told reporters who were hanging around to see the next move in the duel between the two lawyers.

The hearing which had been scheduled on March 13 at the Harrison Town Court did not come off on that day quite the way it had originally been expected.

Instead, there was an extraordinary courtroom confrontation between Westchester County Assistant District Attorney Joseph Abinanti and Town Justice Harvey Fried.

During the confrontation, Aurnou and his colleagues sat quietly by and watched with a somewhat amused air.

The courtroom was packed.

Abinanti rose and requested a three weeks' postponement of the hearing. He told the court the reasons his office desired such an extension of time.

"The issue of intent is a serious issue in this case," he said. "We want the grand jury to decide whether the accused should be charged with second-degree murder or manslaughter."

Judge Fried immediately rejected the request for the postponement.

"Call the first witness," Judge Fried then ordered the prosecutor.

Abinanti said that he was indeed "ready" to proceed, but he indicated that he did not intend to.

Judge Fried pointed out to the prosecutor that the defendant had an "absolute right" to a hearing. Even if, as he acknowledged, it might provide the defense with an "early glimmer" of the kind of evidence that might be used against her, he said that the prosecution need only show that a crime was committed and that there was reason to believe that the defendant committed it.

"If the people file an accusation against [an] individual," Judge Fried continued, "the people must be prepared to back up the accusation immediately. Every crime involves the possibility of a second tragedy, a tragedy to the accused if the accused is not guilty."

Abinanti continued to resist.

Judge Fried, his voice rising with barely concealed anger, said, "I don't know if it's clear that the people are refusing a direct order to proceed!"

Abinanti immediately asked if he could have time to confer with his superior—District Attorney Carl Vergari.

After the confab was over, Abinanti returned to the bench and told the Judge that he requested that the hearing be postponed until "tomorrow"—March 14—at two in the afternoon.

Judge Fried agreed and the session was over.

Later on, Vergari tried to explain the need for the delay to the press, which was clamoring for answers. The point was, if the prosecution *didn't* have a case, why was it trying to delay the moment of truth?

Vergari shook his head. "We simply wanted more time for further investigation. She's out on bail and the time constraint for a speedy hearing does not apply."

He admitted to reporters that there was a possibility that the charge might be reduced to manslaughter, and indicated that another effort would be made the next day to seek a postponement.

"But if Judge Fried orders us to proceed with the probable cause hearing we are prepared to do so. We do not run the risk of charges against this defendant being dismissed."

Aurnou was amused at the whole episode. "Somebody rushed off to charge intentional murder, whereas the charge should be manslaughter at the very most," Aurnou said. "It's apparent that maybe that's being rethought."

It was obvious to reporters that there was an ironic parallel between Abinanti's statements in court and Aurnou's statements out of court.

Aurnou had consistently argued that there was "no intent" in the Jean Harris case.

"It's the first time they've realized they don't know what happened that night," Aurnou said, referring to the night Tarnower was killed.

"First they drag her through the mud," he said, "then go back to find out what happened. It's always easy to say 'love triangle,' but the Tryforos case has nothing to do with it."

But Aurnou would offer no more details to the press.

Jean Harris was in court that day, looking wan and exhausted. She seemed composed, but there were visible bruises on her face and arm.

Aurnou said that she was still in a "state of shock." He told everyone that she was schedduled to check into a Westchester Hospital for both physical and psychological examination.

* * * *

Enter a new character in the strange case of Dr. Herman Tarnower.

Name: O. Steven Frederickson.

Occupation: Private Eye.

Frederickson, president of Manhattan's Venture Investigation and Protection, Inc., was a high-powered, highly-paid private investigator who had been hired by Aurnou.

By now Aurnou knew that his case would depend not on trying to prove that Jean Harris did not shoot Tarnower, but that Tarnower had caused his own death—that is, that Jean Harris was the *victim* rather than the *perpetrator*.

Frederickson was good at his job—gathering facts for the defense case. But because of Jean

Harris's conditon—she was still upset and in shock from the events that had finally caught up with her—Aurnou wanted to use Frederickson as a "bodyguard."

A six-foot, blonde-haired private detective, in his early thirties, Frederickson had started out as an apprentice investigator about twelve years before after a year of service in the U.S. Army in Vietnam.

According to Robert Libbey of Gannett Newspapers, he worked in the usual "sordid areas" of the business at first—matrimonial cases, car repossessions, and serving subpoenas. He got about $70 a week. Eventually he worked his way up until now he was getting $275 a day, with a three-day minimum and expenses.

During the years he was coming up, he decided he enjoyed criminal defense work more than any other kind. "Mainly, violent crime cases."

In New York City circles, Frederickson was noted for his work on the "Subway Slasher" case, during which he even called a press conference to announce that the slasher might be a woman. That was sensational stuff in the city—and the media ate it up.

City detectives did not go for the big ego trip Frederickson was on. "The guy is seeking publicity," muttered one of them darkly.

"I like publicity," Frederickson later acknowledged. "It's good for my business. I like to show people that I get results."

Frederickson had his credits, though. He had nabbed an allegedly crazy killer called the "Tea for Two Bandit" in the summer of 1979 who was terrorizing the New York gay community.

The bandit was known for enticing his victims

to join him for coffee or tea, drugging them, often raping them, and then killing them.

Aurnou wanted Frederickson in those early days of the Harris case to help protect Jean Harris's privacy.

It was at the hearing at the Harrison Town Court that Frederickson made his first appearance on the case—so low-profile that he was almost invisible.

The felony hearing was nearly over in the afternoon and reporters, photographers and cameramen, remembering that Aurnou had flummoxed them the day before by taking his client out the back door, gathered at a side entrance to the courtroom to forestall just such an action.

Inside the courtroom, Town Court Justice Harvey Fried was at that moment recommending after three hours of hearing that the case of Jean Harris go to the grand jury. He did decline to rule on whether or not the day's testimony referred "more to a murder charge or to a manslaughter charge."

"There is enough evidence to conclude that a felony has been committed," Judge Fried said, without mentioning which type of felony he might be referring to.

With that, the hearing ended.

The media was milling about the back door of the Town Court, ready to ask questions of Jean Harris, who today seemed to be in better health.

Inside the court, a large man in a gray suit took Jean Harris by the arm and rapidly led her out through the *front* of the courtroom to the courthouse entrance.

Out back, the herd of media people suddenly realized they were in the wrong place again, and angrily started to follow the defendant. At which point the large man in the gray suit slammed the first set of doors on them, delaying them while they tried to wrest them open.

Out in front of the Town Court a green sedan sat with its motor running. Inside it two men were seated in the front. As the door of the courthouse opened, they leaped out and opened the door of the car.

The big man in the gray suit placed Jean Harris inside, and then leaped into the driver's seat. The green sedan revved up and sped off.

The swarm of reporters circled the car, and two of them claimed that they had been nearly struck by the moving sedan. The driver of the car was O. Steven Frederickson.

Meanwhile, back at the courthouse, the group of media people was stunned by the lightning getaway. Many of them were understandably angry. Reporters and photographers do not pry into people's business because of any innate curiosity on their part. It is their job. If they fail to come up with an interview it means time lost. It also means loss of face and it means trouble back at the studio/newspaper with the boss.

That night Aurnou, according to the Reporter Dispatcher of White Plains, made a personal telephone call to the Gannett Westchester Newspapers to apologize for his investigator's behavior. Aurnou then explained who his aide was.

As for Frederickson, he later said, "The scene at the court house was a fair situation. I couldn't take the chance of having my client surrounded by the press. She might have been hurt by a mike.''

Shortly after that, Jean Harris was admitted to United Hospital in Port Chester for her long-promised rest and psychological evaluation tests.

* * * *

It will be remembered that on Thursday Aurnou and Kelligrew had received subpoenas issued by Vergari's office requiring them to appear before the grand jury on the following Friday with the letter picked up at the Scarsdale Post Office. On Monday, March 17, Aurnou sought a court order to quash the grand jury subpoena.

''We're going to argue in court that the subpoena violates the attorney-client relationship,'' Aurnou said. ''If you gave something to your attorney as privileged, would you want it turned over?''

Aurnou admitted to reporters that the letter might be self-incriminating, but, he said, ''Her psychiatrist has said it would probably help her more than anything else.''

That meant that the psychiatrist as well as Aurnou and Kelligrew must have seen the letter. Nevertheless, a source close to the case said to a New York *Daily News* reporter that the letter would probably not really help the defense much at all.

The arguments in White Plains before Supreme Court Justice Harold Wood on the motion to quash the District Attorney's subpoenas were heard on Tuesday, March 18, rather than Monday.

In his argument, Aurnou said that the letter was subject to the attorney-client privilege, a rule that bars a lawyer from disclosing conversations and certain transactions with his client.

Also, Aurnou said, the subpoena should be quashed because it violated Jean Harris's constitutional protection against self-incrimination and unlawful searches and seizures.

On Vergari's side, he told the court he wanted possession of the letter to determine if it delved into the "state of mind" of the defendant on the day Tarnower was shot to death.

The upshot of the hearing before the State Surpreme Court was that Justice Wood barred the prosecutors from forcing Aurnou to give them the letter on Friday, but referred the matter to State Supreme Court Justice Isaac Rubin and ordered a hearing for Monday, March 24, in White Plains. That was, incidentally, three days after the grand jury was to convene on Friday, March 21.

The duel was beginning to resemble a tennis match, with one point going to the prosecution, and the next going to the defense.

Meanwhile, Vergari scored one on his own. Officials of Fairfax County, Virginia, working in concert with Westchester County officials, searched Jean Harris's red-brick home on the Madeira campus and uncovered eight letters and notes written by Jean Harris.

It was found that five of them were addressed to Tarnower. One was for her sister Mary Margaret Lynch of Shaker Heights, and there were two memos relating to business.

The letters were sent to Westchester to Vergari's office to be made available to the grand jury investigating the Tarnower shooting on Friday.

The grand jury met on Friday, March 21, but Aurnou and Kelligrew did not appear with the letter they had been subpoened to produce; the hearing on whether or not the subpoenas were in effect or not was to be held one court day later, on March 24.

It was composed of 23 members, including four women, and including the grand jury "fore person"—formerly foreman. They went on with their examination of reports and evidence without the letter in question.

The hearing before State Supreme Court Justice Isaac Rubin on Monday was a lengthy one. Aurnou argued that the postal authorities had correctly used Federal law in rejecting the state subpoena for the letter.

Aurnou repeated his arguments that the subpoenas by Vergari had violated his client's rights under the U.S. Constitution against self-incrimination and unreasonable search and seizure of her property.

Also, he claimed that the letter was subject to the attorney-client privilege against disclosure of confidential communications.

Assistant District Attorney Anthony Servino, chief of the appeals and motions bureau, argued that the letter to Tarnower had been written voluntarily.

Also, he said, it was not written in an effort to obtain a lawyer, and therefore the subpoena for it was not unreasonable, vague or broad.

Justice Rubin agreed with Servino, saying that for Aurnou to hand the letter over to the prosecution was not a violation of the rule that Jean

Harris could not be forced to testify against herself.

The reason was that, as Servino had argued, she had voluntarily written the letter in the first place, *before* she was a defendant in a criminal case. If she had written the letter while she was a defendant, only *then* could she claim immunity.

Also, Judge Rubin said, the seizure of the property—meaning the proposed seizure of the letter by the prosecutors—was not an unreasonable act because the subpoena was specific and not "burdensome on the defense attorney."

Justice Rubin then said that no attorney-client privilege applied to the situation because Jean Harris had not written the letter to hire an attorney or communicate with him about her case.

He then ordered Aurnou to appear before the grand jury at 11 a.m. on the following day, March 25, with the letter.

Aurnou said he would seek to have the order "stayed," or, in layman's terms, delayed, by a justice of the Appellate Division of the State Supreme Court.

If that attempt failed, Aurnou said, he would be reduced to two choices: he could either produce the letter or he could risk contempt of court.

Time was running out for Aurnou, but nevertheless, next morning, he sought a stay of the order to present the letter. Justice James D. Hopkins, of the Appellate Division of the State Supreme Court, rejected Aurnou's appeal that same morning.

However, several important decisions had already been made in the meantime. The grand jury had been meeting for two days, March 21 and 24.

On the late afternoon of March 24, the grand jury had voted to indict Jean Harris on a charge of second-degree murder in the death of Dr. Herman Tarnower, saying that it appeared that she did indeed intend to kill her longtime friend by shooting him four times with a .32-caliber revolver.

The grand jury had been fully aware of all the options, according to Vergari, meaning that it had been aware of proposing a lesser manslaughter charge as well as the second-degree murder charge.

The grand jury also indicted Jean Harris on two counts of gun possession. In one she was accused of intending to use a gun unlawfully against Tarnower, and in the other she was charged with simple possession. No date was set for her formal arraignment on those charges.

With the indictment handed up to Judge John C. Couzens, of Westchester County Court, at 10 a.m. on the morning of March 25, one hour before the deadline at which Aurnou was to appear before the grand jury with the letter, Vergari decided to inform Justice Hopkins of the Appellate Division of that fact.

"We told the judge the indictment was in," Vergari said. "We had decided we weren't going to hang around waiting for the letter."

And so Justice Hopkins simply rejected Aurnou's appeal on the grounds that the subpoena had now become moot—that is, that the grand jury had already brought in an indictment of the defendant on the higher charge of second-degree murder.

In the end, the ping-pong game over the letter

turned out to be irrelevant to the issue. Unfortunately for Aurnou, the grand jury had come up with an indictment of the defendant on a higher charge than he had hoped for.

Nevertheless, it would now be up to the prosecution to prove that Jean Harris had acted "with intent to cause death." If that could be proved, then the defendant could get as much as twenty-five years to life in prison.

However, the trial jury could find that she did so "under extreme emotional disturbance," and return a lesser verdict of manslaughter.

By now Aurnou's case seemed to be clearer.

"Our defense," he said, as reported in *The New York Times*, "is that Jean Harris did not intend to kill, so there's no murder and therefore nothing to reduce. She did not intend to harm him, let alone kill him. Her intent was to do away with herself."

Aurnou announced that his client was now under constant care. He did say that he was hopeful that she could soon get away and become a "house guest under 24-hour watch."

Vergari was exuberant. He termed the grand jury's action as vindication over an investigation that had been overshadowed by the excitement of the case itself—and as a counterpoint to the sympathy and support expressed by the public for Jean Harris.

Aurnou countered with the claim that Jean Harris was the *victim* in the case. He kept insisting that the case had nothing to do with Lynne Tryforos—that is, that there was no jealousy involved in Jean Harris's actions.

Nevertheless, Vergari said that the letter, which was still in Aurnou's possession, was relevant to the coming trial, and that he would continue to seek it. He could do that through pre-trial discovery proceedings as the trial itself came closer.

The trial would not be held, according to most speculation, until about six to eight months from the time of the indictment.

Aurnou's reaction to the events was a simple one:

"Vergari got his indictment, and I've got the letter," he said.

At this juncture, there was only one more legal move before the setting of the trial for Jean Harris.

On March 28, Jean Harris was formally arraigned on a charge of second-degree murder in a White Plains court before Westchester County Judge John Couzens.

On that day, she appeared well-groomed, according to news reports of the arraignment, and seemed "rested afer a ten-day stay" at United Hospital in Port Chester where she had been undergoing mental and physical treatment.

She was "calm and rested," and appeared "in sharp contrast to the distraught woman" who first appeared on television screens after her first court appearance on March 12.

During the arraignment, police reports were entered as prosecution material, with Vergari's office saying that the killing resulted from a love triangle when Tarnower ended his fourteen-year affair with Jean Harris in favor of his assistant, Lynne Tryforos.

The arraignment was brief, but the documents that were handed over the Aurnou were quite detailed and extensive. Some of the material had not yet been made public—but was now revealed to the press.

Judge Couzens continued Jean Harris's bail and gave her permission to leave Westchester County over the weekend to return to Virginia to pick up some personal belongings at Madeira School.

She was fingerprinted and then left with Aurnou through a basement exit of the courthouse.

13

The Aftermath

During this prolonged period of legal maneuvering by the prosecution and defense, there were unusual public repercussions even for a murder case of its obvious importance and impact.

First, the fact that Dr. Herman Tarnower was a best-selling author pushed the case into the highest category of news possible in both print and electronic media.

Second, the fact that the suspect was a *bona fide*, established, listed member of the Social Register in Washington tended to make the case twice as exciting as it might have been had she been an ordinary housewife.

Third, the fact that she was a socialite who was headmistress at a prestigious school like Madeira in Virginia, attended by the children of the power elite in the nation's capital, gave the case a most unusual dimension.

Fourth, the amazing fact that both the suspect and the victim were practicing a lifestyle that had become almost commonplace among the young and the mod middle class added a fillip of sociological excitement to the crime.

Of course, there *was* a beautiful woman in the case—Lynne Tryforos.

Sex. Money. Prestige. Power.

The press went raving mad over the case.

Tarnower was immediately tagged the "diet doc" and Jean Harris became the "socialite" and "headmistress."

Sadly enough, Hi Tarnower's rueful predictions had come true: "I'm a good cardiologist, but I'll probably be known as the doctor who developed the Scarsdale Diet."

Luckily, he never knew that he would be immortalized in the tabloids as a "diet doc" in three-inch headlines during a good part of March, 1980.

The New York *Daily News'* DIET DOC SLAIN, NAB SOCIALITE IN DOC'S SLAYING were mild headlines compared to some that appeared. HEAD OF POSH GIRLS' SCHOOL IS TARNOWER SUSPECT, SLAIN DOC IN LOVE TRIANGLE, was a *New York Post* headline.

Even the staid *New York Times* ran the story on the front page: " 'Scarsdale Diet' Doctor Slain; Headmistress Charged." "Mystery of Other Woman to Who Came to Dinner . . ." said the *New York Post* in a subhead.

Things were happening so fast that the copywriters weren't able to check many of their facts. *The New York Times* had Lynne Tryforos as "Lynn Dryfaros," and Henri van der Vreken as "Andre" van der Vreken; that, in spite of the fact that their own food editor, Craig Claibourne, had run a story about Tarnower in a 1979 column that mentioned Henri van der Vreken accurately. In fact, van der Vreken appeared variously as Henry, Andre, and Henri those first few days. His wife, Suzanne, appeared as Suzenne several places for no apparent reason.

Joel Aurnou appeared as Arnew, Arnow, Arnou, Aurnew, in a variety of different spellings. For Aurnou, spelling his name wrong was nothing new. As a matter of fact, his listing in the White Plains telephone directory is not only under Aurnou, his real name with its proper spelling, but also Arnou, a possible misspelling.

"That's for clients who can't spell," he said once when asked why he preferred the double listing including a misspelling to a single accurate listing.

The .32-caliber Harrington & Richardson revolver appeared in several places as a .32-caliber Smith & Wesson. Jean Struven Harris appeared as Jean Strueven Harris in several stories.

But no one made a mistake about one of the most confusing similarities in the story. Harrison Police Chief William Harris always appeared as William Harris rather than Harrison, and Jean Harris always appeared as Jean Harris rather than Jean Harrison, and the Harrington & Richardson revolver did not appear as the Harrison & Richardson revolver.

The victim was almost without exception identified as Tarnower, although an occasional typographic error had it Tarnover. However, his nickname, "Hi," was erroneously reported as "Hy" in several instances.

The Scarsdale Medical Center appeared as that—its correct name—or the Scarsdale Medical Group, which was the name of the clinic formed by the two of the doctors who eventually made up half of the Scarsdale Medical Center, the men themselves being the Scarsdale Medical Group. However, the Center was occasionally called the Group; mail addressed to the Group went to the Center.

The Scarsdale Medical Center immediately closed its doors until Tarnower's funeral, but the place that was most upset by the arraignment of Jean Harris for second-degree murder was Madeira School.

* * * *

The shock waves over the news of Tarnower's death and Jean Harris's implication in it were so far-reaching and shattering that the 74-year old school held a press conference on Tuesday "amid tight security," as one report had it, to announce that Jean Harris intended to resign as headmistress.

"We are most disturbed by the unfortunate events that affect Mrs. Harris," said Alice W. Faulkner, the president of the school. "We hope," she continued, "[the slaying] will have no effect on the school. We feel we have a very fine, very strong, very healthy school."

Faulkner said in her announcement at the press conference: "There has been a great outpouring of support for Mrs. Harris."

But disturbing memories of the past were immediately raised by the spectre of the "headmistress as murderess." In fact, the *Washington Post* again recapped the 1973 story of the slaying of the 14-year-old student from Arlington in the sex-related murder that made such grisly reading in the press. The death, the story said, "troubled students and faculty at the school for several years."

And now—this!

Laura Gill, president of the day school student body—that is, the students who did not live on the campus but commuted daily from their homes around McLean—was quoted in the press as saying, "No matter what happens to [Jean Harris] I am going to continue to believe in her."

And Sonya Knight, president of the boarding school students—that is, those students who lived on the campus rather than those who commuted—said that Jean Harris had helped the students draw up an honor code for the school.

"The code basically encompassed stealing, cheating and lying. Each student was on their own, it wasn't a West Point deal," she pointed out.

"She was very easy to talk to," Knight added. "She lived on campus and her house was always open to any student at any time, day or night. In the night, you could walk in and talk to her without hesitation.

"If a student was willing to sit down and talk to her, she could find a solution to a problem. Most of the students respected her very much, and she constantly expressed how much she respected the students."

One parent of a student at Madeira said, "She was an excellent headmistress who was doing well at an extremely taxing job."

"This is not the kind of person to murder someone," said a colleague of Jean Harris's. "It must be a dreadful mistake. She was a perfectly delightful woman. Listen to me, speaking in the past tense as though she had died. Oh, this is terrible!"

A prominent alumna, who requested anonymity, said, "Jean Harris worked enormously hard for the school in a position of extreme difficulty. She was proud of the fact that she had been able to attract younger teachers to the school, while at the same time seeking to set a higher standard of values."

"She was a charming woman," the parent of one student remarked. "But she was very strict. She didn't put up with anything and we found that very attractive."

Some of the girls at Madeira said Jean Harris could be cold and severe at times, but all who were willing to discuss her said they felt her incapable of killing anyone.

A former colleague of Harris, Rosalie Whittaker of Trenton, N.J., described Jean Harris as brilliant, quiet, and "given to moods of darkness. Don't misquote me, now. I'm not talking about anything like murder. But she was morose sometimes, like perhaps she was depressed."

"It's just too bizarre," said one student. "Freaky, like something out of Agatha Christie. It's not fun, though. I feel a little sick."

Within two days, however, Madeira School had weathered the storm of media people who swarmed there for the press conference and interviewed any of the students who might be there during the three-week spring vacation.

Kathleen G. Johnson, academic dean, was appointed acting headmistress of Madeira School when Jean Harris telephoned her resignation from the job on Wednesday. Johnson was interviewed by a *Washington Post* reporter.

Privately, she admitted that she was aware that Jean Harris *was* "friendly" with Hi Tarnower. But she was actually unaware of the depth of that friendship.

"He was her family doctor, and I thought her good friend as well," Johnson told the reporter.

Johnson remembered what Lucy Madeira, the school's founder and namesake, had said about crises—"Keep calm at the very center of your being."

"Of course," Johnson said, "Miss Madeira didn't expect a disaster like this. But she expected you to cope, regardless, and we are. We are sending out report cards today."

* * * *

On Thursday, March 13, the body of Dr. Herman Tarnower was put to rest after funeral services at the Larchmont Temple in Westchester County. Some 400 mourners appeared at the services, including relatives and the many friends of the eminent cardiologist.

In their mink coats, their jewelry and their chauffeur-driven limousines, they seemed to fit right in with the heady atmosphere of material success and high-society glamour that surrounded Tarnower through the later years of his life.

Rabbi H. Leonard Poller conducted the service that was notable for its lack of the ritual that is normally associated with a Jewish funeral.

The body lay in a closed, shiny, reddish wooden mahogany coffin. Large sprays of white roses had been placed at either side of the casket at the front of the temple. There were approximately 70 roses, one for each year of Tarnower's life.

There was only one Hebrew prayer, uttered first in Hebrew and then translated into English:

"His life's song was broken off halfway. How grieved we are the loss of this poet of a person, this skilled physician."

During the 25-minute service, Rabbi Poller talked of Tarnower as a man who lived out the ideals of Judaism as described by Albert Einstein: he pursued knowledge for its own sake; he displayed an almost fanatical love of justice; and he had desire for personal independence.

He described Tarnower as an "eternal student," a physician of the first rank "whose brooding mind made him ask for answers to questions about the unknown."

Rabbi Poller did mention in passing the situation that led to the death of Tarnower.

"No one in full or reasonable control of self would dare attempt to reduce him of that personal independence. Perhaps one senselessly tried to do that at the last.

"Dr. Tarnower was a person whose determined spirit of independence made him be a servant of the larger world and did so, perhaps, at a continuous high cost, even to the end of his days."

Although there had been little snow during the winter of 1979-80 in Westchester County, light snow drifted outside the synagogue as the rabbi gave his eulogy.

Tarnower's sister Pearl, known as "Billie," was the only surviving direct kin of Tarnower's generation.

Among those attending the funeral, as reported in the press, were New York State Senator Roy Goodman, Republican of Manhattan who lived near Tarnower in Purchase; investment banker John Loeb Jr., also of Purchase; Benjamin Berkey, head of Berkey Photo; architect Robert Jacobs of New York City and Pawling; and Samm Sinclair Baker, Tarnower's co-author.

Lynne Tryforos was present at the funeral, although she was not immediately noticed.

Mourners did not discuss Tarnower's romantic life, but many of them said that he was an exceedingly masculine person—"a man's man" who liked to hunt, fish, and play golf.

One of his patients said, "There were always a lot of women around him. He had many women friends."

Tarnower was buried in Mount Hope Cemetery, Hastings-on-Hudson. The burial was a private ceremony, with only 20 persons, close relatives and friends, attending the brief service.

* * * *

On March 26, Dr. Herman Tarnower's will was filed in Westchester County Surrogate's Court. It was dated January 21, 1980—having been made out, surprisingly enough, only about six weeks before his death. His estate, in legal language, was stated to be "over $1 million."

The will had been made out by Tarnower's cousin, Leo Dikman of Pleasantville, an attorney with offices in Queens, New York. There were two witnesses to Tarnower's signing of the will on January 21: Dr. Roderick Granzen of White Plains, a partner in the Scarsdale Medical Center and Dr. James L. Carvelas, another partner at the Center.

No reason had been given for the changes that Tarnower made in his will at the time, according to Granzen and Carvelas. Granzen said Tarnower was a "private, personal man who never discussed his personal business with anybody."

There were a large number of beneficiaries, but the bulk of the estate went to a handful of close relatives—and two surprise non-relatives.

The big house in Purchase and the grounds surrounding it, which had been evaluated at about $500,000, went to Tarnower's sister, Pearl Tarnower Schwartz, who was to receive $1,000 in cash in addition to the property.

But the two most fascinating allocations of money were those made out to Jean Harris and Lynne Tryforos—the two women who obviously were the focal points in Tarnower's later years.

A bequest of $220,000 went to Jean Struven Harris. Interestingly enough, if she were to be convicted of the second-degree murder charges she faced, she would not collect the inheritance. New York State law says that it is illegal to profit from a crime.

Even if she were to be convicted of either of the two charges of manslaughter, she would not collect a penny either—since manslaughter is a crime as well as murder.

In the event that Jean Harris were to be convicted of any degree of crime in relation to Tarnower, the $220,000 would be forfeited and would be redistributed in the "residue" of the estate—about which more in a moment.

A bequest of $200,000 went to Lynne Tryforos.

On March 28, the New York *Daily News* headlined the story: "Diet Doc's Will: 420G for Lovers."

Tarnower was apparently not, as one friend had asserted, a "one-woman man" at all. He had obviously been unable to reject Jean Harris totally—if he had even been prompted to reject her partially—and had been just as unable to substitute Lynn Tryforos completely in her place.

Why he had added the $20,000 to what would have been equal shares to both his "women" was not obvious.

Tarnower had certainly *not* written off Jean Harris. Nor had he "written in" Lynne Tryforos, either.

His relationship with both of these women was almost equal, at least in his mind they must have been at the time in January when he had drawn up a new will.

In addition to the $200,000 he gave Lynne Tryforos, he included her two daughters, Laura and Electra, in his bequests, giving each of them $20,000 on the condition that they attend college and enroll before their twentieth birthdays.

They would be paid a portion of an amount of the $190,000 college trust fund Tarnower set up for the six sons and daughters of his nephews and nieces and for the two Tryforos daughters. The will stipulated that money from the college trust fund would be paid to them each year only while they attended college to cover their expenses.

Four of Tarnower's nieces and a nephew were given outright gifts of cash and were also to share in what was called the "residue" of Tarnower's estate—that is, everything that might come in to the estate later on that was not already allocated to anyone in the will.

For example, "residue" would include all the money in royalties received from the sale of Tarnower's Scarsdale Diet book. The split of this revenue was divided among four people:

● 40 percent of the residue was to go to Debbie Schwartz Raizes. In addition, she was allocated $40,000 outright upon probate of the will.

● 20 percent was to go to Cindy Schwartz Johnson. In addition, she was allocated $40,000 outright.

● 20 percent was to go to Peter Nisselsen. In addition, he was allocated $40,000 outright.

● 20 percent was to go to Roberta Pascal Patten. In addition, she was allocated $40,000 outright.

The "residue" was a possible goldmine for the four lucky recipients. At the time of his death, the diet book had reportedly grossed more than $11 million in hardcover sales alone, with sales exceeding 750,000. However, the paperback rights could more than double that figure in the next few years.

One odd result of the dramatic death of Dr. Herman Tarnower was the sudden resurgence of sales of his Scarsdale Diet book. For twelve weeks the paperback edition of the book had been running very well in the Number Three spot—great, but not sensational.

But quite suddenly in the middle of March, the sales figures increased substantially, pushing the book into the Number One sales spot. Bantam Books reported going back to press for 200,000 more copies, bringing the total in print to close to 1,400,000 copies.

Publishing experts usually figure January and May as the traditional months when America feel the urge to buy diet books. (Something about New Year's resolutions, perhaps, and the post-Lent season?) This mid-March jump was unprecedented, but hardly inexplicable.

A lot of people in the country had been apparently unaware of the book and of the Scarsdale Diet. But when news of the murder appeared everywhere, many people discovered the Diet as well as the previous existence of Dr. Herman Tarnower.

Such a posthumous rise in sales for authors is not unusual. Just after Jacqueline Susann and Helen Van Slyke died, there was, according to publications mavens, a comparable rise in demand for their novels.

Net royalties of the Scarsdale Diet Book, of course, would be much smaller than the $11 million mentioned (which represents the gross receipts)—and it is also logical to assume that a percentage split of the take went to co-author Samm Sinclair Baker. Nevertheless, the "residue" would be an extremely healthy amount in the future.

The Scarsdale Medical Center building housing the prestigious Scarsdale Medical Group, which was Tarnower's property, would remain under the control of the will's executors, who would be empowered to continue to lease it to the eight remaining doctors who were partners in the group practice.

The doctors were granted a "right of first refusal" for up to five years, should the executors decide to sell the property or if the members of the group practice wished to purchase it. There was no estimate as to the value of the property.

Other bequests were as follows:

● To each of the sons and daughters of his nieces and nephew: $20,000 apiece outright.

● To Henri and Suzanne van der Vreken, Tarnower's housekeepers: each would receive $32,000—$2,000 for each of the 16 years they had worked for him.

● To Phyllis Rogers, his long-time secretary: $20,000.

● To Doris McKenzie, a "loyal employee": $5,000.

● To Dr. John Cannon, Tarnower's associate at the Scarsdale Medical Center, who is sasid to have assisted in the development of the Scarsdale Diet: $10,000.

● To the Westchester Heart Association: $15,000.

● To Leo Dikman, a cousin, $20,000.

● To Samuel Tarnower, an uncle, $20,000.

● To Gerda Stedman, a friend: $10,000.

Although the value of Tarnower's estate was put at "over $1 million," it was estimated that the actual value of the doctor's estate was closer to $2 million and maybe even more. That would include the proceeds from the diet book, his

Purchase home, its furnishings and its grounds, and the building and equipment of the Scarsdale Medical Center.

Dr. Roderick Granzen, who witnessed the signing of the will, said that he had not known of any of the provisions of the will at the time he saw Tarnower sign the document. But he felt that the allocations had been thought out quite carefully.

"He was a very intelligent man and he always had a reason for what he put in an agreement or a will," Granzen said.

14

The Reconstruction

The battle lines were drawn.

The prosecution had its case drawn up in part. At least the District Attorney had already put together enough evidence for the grand jury to proceed on a charge.

It was obvious that the prosecution was basing its case—that Jean Harris had come to Dr. Herman Tarnower's house "with intent" to kill him—on the motive behind that intent.

It would seem that there would be stress on the alleged romantic triangle that occupied the heart specialist in his last years.

It was up to the District Attorney's staff to prove that Lynne Tryforos had in fact replaced Jean Harris in Hi Tarnower's affections. In turn, by being displaced, Jean Harris had then become jealous of the other woman.

Then the prosecution would have to prove that Jean Harris had become angered at Tarnower, rather than at the other woman, and had decided to kill him.

The District Attorney's men would have to prove that she went to his bedroom and killed him. If they could prove this, they would be able to convict her of second-degree murder.

But it wouldn't be all that easy. There were

certain facts that did not actually bear out the scenario of the prosecution's case. For example, even though Jean Harris had asked the police who was at dinner the night Tarnower died, she apparently did not mention Lynne Tryforos by name.

It seemed obvious that she was thinking of Lynne Tryforos, but even so she might not have been referring to her at all. The prosecution would have to establish beyond a reasonable doubt that Jean Harris was jealous of Lynne Tryforos.

If Jean Harris had been intent on killing Tarnower, she would probably have entered the bedroom, confronted him, and shot him. Instead of that, there had been an obvious struggle. Tarnower had got his licks in on her—the bruised mouth and the reported bruised eye and the long bruise on the arm all attested to these facts.

If he had seen her with the gun, he would have tried to wrest it from her. He would not have hit her in the mouth and arm; he might have hit her on the wrist. He would have been totally intent on the gun. The fact that Jean Harris bore bruises on the mouth and face meant that she had not gone into the room with the gun in her hand and immediately carried out her intent.

Why did the two of them argue?

Those problems would have to be surmounted by the prosecution.

* * * *

The defense had its case already drawn up in part, too. Aurnou in his mind had a pretty fair idea of how he would handle the material in order to give the jury enough evidence to decide whether or not Jean Harris intended to kill Tarnower.

It was obvious that the defense was basing its case—that Jean Harris had come to Dr. Herman Tarnower's house with the intention of having him kill her—on the statements that she had already made and were now a matter of court record, and also on the material in the long letter she had written to Tarnower on the day of his death.

That meant that Aurnou would put emphasis on Jean Harris's relationship with Hi Tarnower, especially on Tarnower's apparent recent rejection of her as his long-time companion.

It was up to Aurnou to prove that Lynne Tryforos's attentions to Tarnower had little to do with Jean Harris's personal feelings about Tarnower. What Aurnou wanted to prove would be that Tarnower rejected her—dropped her, as it were—and treated her badly in those last months of his life.

Aurnou saw Jean Harris as the "victim" rather than the "aggressor" or "perpetrator" of the crime. That is what he told the press.

If he choose that approach, he would have to demonstrate that Jean Harris felt that her life had begun to disintegrate because of Tarnower's growing indifference to her. Then, he might have to show that Jean Harris's despair had been aggravated by Tarnower's coldness. He might suggest that she felt that she had nowhere to go, no one to see, no one at all—after spending fourteen years of her life as Tarnower's constant companion—free translation, "lover."

He would have to prove that Jean Harris loved Tarnower; that she would not and could not *think* of killing him. "Tarnower never in his life had to fight off this lady. This lady would have died for him."

And, most difficult of all, he would have to prove that Jean Harris had taken a handgun she had purchased several years before, had put it in its box—loaded—had taken it to Tarnower's bedroom that night in order to have him kill her!

That wouldn't be easy to prove. There were certain facts that didn't tie in.

For example, the cold truth was that Jean Harris had allegedly shot five bullets at Tarnower—and four of them had hit him! Was this the act of a woman who had intended to have him kill her? Assuming the intent, how had it all been turned around at the last moment so that *she* was shooting *him*?

Another difficult portion of the defense's case was the simple fact of the .32 caliber Harrington & Richardson revolver. It had been purchased by Jean Harris. Why? She was not an avid hunter like Tarnower. She was not a target shooter. She was not particularly afraid for her life on the sedate Madeira campus—in spite of the 1973 murder on the grounds.

She had bought the gun and she had bought a brand new box of bullets for it. She had set out on that Monday in March with it in her car, loaded. These facts would be hard to reconcile with the premise that she was going up to Tarnower's house to try to persuade *him* to kill *her*.

But of course neither of these cumbersome facts would mean anything if Aurnou could prove that Jean Harris came up to Purchase in a distraught frame of mind, did not know what she was doing when she burst into the house, and had no idea of what she was arguing about with Tarnower, and did not know that she was shooting him when she did so.

But that legal battle lay in the future.

And that battle would be ringed with legal maneuvers of one kind or another—some to suppress evidence, others to bring out evidence. Although the adversary relationship between prosecution and defense is an excellent way to protect the rights of the defendant, it may not, in the long run, be conducive to revealing the truth and the whole truth in all its pristine glory.

What the average person always wanted to know right away was:

What really happened in the bedroom that night?

Disregarding all nuances of legality, like the finer shades of intent, purpose and motivation, and disregarding all hair-line rules of evidence, exactly what did happen in that room?

* * * *

Anyone who has read this far in the story of the relationship between Hi Tarnower and Jean Harris will know for sure that a number of unexplained things happened in that room—or, at least, seemed to have happened.

For instance, when and if Hi Tarnower saw Jean Harris starting to shoot him with the handgun in her possession, why didn't he grab it from her and throw it away?

If she intended to go up to Tarnower's house and kill him, why did she write him a long letter and post it registered mail so that it would be in his possession *after she had killed him*?

But if she intended to go up to Tarnower's house to persuade him to kill her, why didn't she take the letter along with her?

People do act illogically, of course. Many of them act illogically to a greater degree when they are involved in a bitter confrontation—as were Jean Harris and Hi Tarnower.

But the two problems in logic are baffling ones.

Let's first explore the question regarding Tarnower's actions as he was about to be shot to death.

Here was a man who had spent time in Africa on big-game safaris. Here was a man who knew guns and knew how to use them. Here was a man who was definitely a "man's man," as he was often called. Here was a man who excelled at conquest and the exertion of power.

He was apparently confronted by a woman who was obviously beside herself. Whether or not she asked him to kill her makes no difference at all in our consideration of Tarnower and his actions.

Suppose she did ask him to kill her. He would immediately say, No, he would not. "Get out of here; you're crazy," is a thing he might have said, certainly. Jean Harris says that he did say just that.

Suppose she did not ask him to shoot her. Suppose she simply announced that she was going to kill him. What would he say then? He would respond that she couldn't be serious; he would try to tease her out of her state of anger.

But in either case—if she asked him to kill her,

or if she told him she was going to kill him—he would see the gun we assume she held in her hand. He would wonder if it was loaded, but only for an instant. He was a man who had been in military service. He was a man who had killed big game. He was a man who spent hours fishing, tracking other elusive quarry.

Loaded or not, a handgun must be considered a lethal weapon.

Instinctively, it would seem, Tarnower should have gone for the gun, to wrest it aside, or throw it away. At least get it out of her hand.

Why did he not?

For the sake of argument, let's assume that he did rush for her gun. Let's assume that Jean Harris panicked when she saw him move toward her and fired—either with intent, or without intent, it does not matter. Let's assume she fired and the bullet went through Tarnower's right hand—as that hand was in the process of grabbing the gun. That action fits the facts.

But if this actually happened, the very next move on Tarnower's part, instinctively, if for no other reason, would be to withdraw his right hand and slash at the gun with his left, trying to dislodge it.

If he had done so, he most certainly would have disarmed Jean Harris. He was a strong man.

He did neither, and was shot—not once, but four more times!

It is simply not easy to understand how this man who knew guns, who was a military person, who had hunting experience, could let someone else shoot at him in his bedroom—even someone like Jean Harris, an intimate—without putting up a fight that would have dislodged the gun from her hand and prevented his death.

He did *not* take the gun from her. Because he did not, he died.

He could have been surprised, of course. He could have been half asleep. He could have stood there, listening to her for a moment without realizing that she had a gun in her hand.

But that is not right, either—because Jean Harris was bruised from blows presumably sustained in an altercation with Tarnower. When did their fight occur? When did he punch her in the mouth? Where was the gun when they fought each other?

It was not a surprise encounter, and—bang! bang! bang! bang! The verbal argument occurred. The physical encounter occurred. He saw the gun. Why did he ignore it?

* * * *

Now, to explore the problem of Jean Harris and the letter she wrote to Hi Tarnower—a letter that would be delivered at least a day or two after the time it was posted.

In a way, the writing of that letter makes the least sense of anything that occurred on the crucial day.

If Jean Harris intended to go up to Purchase, enter the Tarnower house, and try to persuade him to kill her—why did she post the letter at all? If she wanted him to read it, why didn't she take it along with her in the car? Why did she write it at all, if she wanted to have it out with him face to face?

If Jean Harris intended to go up to Purchase

to kill him, why did she post the letter at all? He would have been dead long before it was delivered to his office.

The truth of the matter is that the two actions—that of writing the letter and that of driving up to Purchase—negate each other. If she was going to Purchase, why did she feel she should write a letter to Tarnower?

One way to resolve those seemingly contradictory facts is to speculate that Jean Harris had a change of mind between the time she was scribbling out the letter and the notes to relatives and friends and the time she started out in her car.

What change of mind?

A sequence of events, of course, purely speculative—as everything must be at this point about Jean Harris and Hi Tarnower.

We have been exposed to a definite fact—that Jean Harris thought she would be dead soon and had written notes to relatives to that effect. Suppose she had decided something on Monday—quite probably after the morning meeting she attended at wh' ... she seemed quite rational and calm and quite probably after she had ended the telephone call she put in to Westchester County in the middle of the day—that she was going to kill herself.

Suppose she then wrote notes to her relatives and to Tarnower, telling him that she was going to finish what he had in effect begun . . . her own destruction.

Suppose then that she put the gun she had brought in the box and took it out to the car and drove off to a lonely part of the countryside to do away with herself.

But despite her resolution and despite the fact

that she did not want to live, suppose she was simply unable to carry out her plan. At that point she might have remembered the letters she had written and the special delivery that she had posted to Tarnower.

They would of course be but meaningless ramblings if she could not kill herself. Suppose she was beside herself with chagrin over her inability to act. Suppose she then drove the car up to Purchase.

As she drove, she might have conceived a new plan—one which might have seemed logical to her in her emotional stress—of giving the gun to Tarnower and letting *him* finish her off. If he wouldn't accept her any more, he could at least help her accomplish her one aim—death.

Then, of course, once she arrived at Tarnower's house and spoke to him, he could have reacted in a fashion that outraged her. It can be guessed that he possibly laughed at her, scoffing at her for her naiveté. Why should he kill her? He didn't hate her. He might have said he loved her. He might have told her that the two of them had too many good memories for him to do away with her.

Or perhaps he simply turned his back on her.

Being rejected was one thing. Jean Harris had been rejected by him already. But suppose now he was again rejecting her—in a most crucial moment of her life. He would in effect be turning away from her when she was asking him for help.

* * * *

As we have noted, Tarnower was a man of extreme intelligence, of a strong character, of a self-assurance that was seen by some as being rank egocentricity.

He was as emotionless as a machine. He did not suffer from inhibition the way most people do. He believed in himself and in his manifold talents to a degree that would frighten most people.

His life work was medicine, and he loved to treat people. It is interesting to realize that he treated them quite probably not because he loved them as fellow human beings but because their disabilities and their unhealthy conditions were challenges that stimulated him.

We cannot know this for a fact; but in studying his relationship with the people he worked with and knew, it seems fairly reasonable.

His interest in diet once again exemplifies the type of challenge that he loved best. His mind was fundamentally mathematics- and science-oriented. He knew all the scientific moves. He knew, for example, what foods people could eat to lose weight. He also knew enough about psychology to know that people did not always follow rules the way he himself did. So he erected built-in fail-safes in his diet—so his dieters would follow enough of the rules to lose the weight they wished. His diet became a kind of game he played with his dieters.

We also know that Tarnower was an avid hunter. Again, he considered the fish he was angling for, the animal he was stalking, as quarry—not as individual animal beings. In effect, it was again a game. Perhaps he considered his quarry as nothing more than a symbol—a target for him to shoot.

Gamesmanship may have been the key to Tarnower's character. Perhaps he treated patients in such a way that a cure would give him a certain number of invisible points; a setback would put him back to square one; a failure was the loss of the whole match.

Certainly he understood the gamesmanship involved in creating a proper cultural background against which he could feature himself. Certainly he knew exactly the right objets d'art, artifacts, foods, wines, in sum the right things in the right place for the perfect effect.

His delight was in things, in subtle nuances, in taste, in appearances.

One of his early acquaintances in college said an odd thing.

"He couldn't relate to women."

It was an astute observation, obviously. But it could have gone further. Perhaps what she should have said was, "He couldn't relate to people."

There are many others who said he was a "man's man," but perhaps even so he didn't really relate to men either. He was described by many people as a "martinet," a "task-master," and so on. His military experience and bearing have been commented on already.

One proof of the statement—"He couldn't relate to women"—that is quite obvious is the fact that he never married. That did not mean that he never had affairs with women. Nor did it mean that he never used women in all in the conventional ways men use women.

From what we can gather, Tarnower had a rather congenial contempt for most of the people he met. There were so very few top-grade intellects like his, so few men with such excellent taste, such self-reliance, such *style*. In a way, people around him were not much more to him, perhaps, than the animals he chased on his hunting forays. Perhaps, like these animals, the people he met in his everyday life, his patients, his dinner guests, were simply symbols, too. They were, perhaps, symbols of his stock in trade: medicine.

"He couldn't relate to people," we have said.

Rage, hate, envy, jealousy, affection—love? Perhaps these human emotions were remote to his sphere of existence.

He was used to having people do what he told them to do. One of his partners once said, "I'd never think of not following his advice to the letter."

He expected total obedience.

Yet the woman who had wanted to share his life for fourteen years suddenly turned on him one night.

Perhaps he turned his back to wait for her to cool down. Emotion was too silly a thing to get worked up about, and when his back was turned, perhaps that was when she shot him—enraged that he would not *relate* to her despair.

Tarnower's fatal flaw was perhaps that he was not able to relate to other people as *human beings* rather than as patients, golf and dinner companions, and bedmates. They were symbols, to participate with, not flesh and blood, emotional individuals. He may have died because he was not able to understand the inner workings of another human being.

Perhaps. It is all speculation.

Tarnower died because he did not fight

back—hard enough, quick enough, alertly enough.

* * * *

If Jean Harris indeed shot Tarnower, there is a great deal of question as to why she did it, and in exactly what mood she was in when she did it.

She, like Tarnower, was a product of a wealthy family, and she, like him, also had a superior intellect. Perhaps hers was not quite so rare and well-developed as his, but she was certainly a superior scholar with a very high I.Q.

She had known guns from her youth. With a father who was a military careerist, she had certainly been exposed to them. She knew of their uses and of their danger.

Jean Harris viewed people in somewhat the same way that Tarnower did, but she related to them better than he. Even though her marriage had failed, she had successfully and alone brought up two children.

Her character was strong, her convictions powerful, her code rigid. She had a direct way about her. She let nothing stop her from succeeding at whatever she set out to do.

She was aloof, and austere, but, unlike Tarnower, she understood people and the things that motivate them. She loved to mold character—particularly the unformed characters of the young women who were in her classes and under her guidance when she was headmistress, and she was very direct when she did not like what someone was doing. She effected punishment quickly and severely. In her training she was as much a martinet at Tarnower. When someone crossed her, she reacted quickly and some times sharply.

She was not one to sit back wistfully and try to rationalize a particular transgression. She stepped in immediately, went directly to the heart of the matter, and inflicted punishment where it was due.

The raids she directed against the Madeira dormitories are a case in point. Some of the students considered her too hard.

Her life was not quite as smooth as Tarnower's. She lost out on an important promotion when she was starting out in teaching. She lost another job when Thomas School folded. She had trouble instilling a sense of integrity in the students at Madeira.

Like many people who, on the surface, are as placid as a deep glacial lake high in the mountains, she was apparently seething inside. In the midst of a quiet conversation, when things did not go her way, she could become highly emotional.

We do not know what her mood was when she entered Tarnower's bedroom that night. We do not know if she came there to kill him, or to have him kill her. We do know that she went into the room and that she must have had the gun with her because it was fired in that room and then taken down to the car again.

We can assume she was either distraught when she confronted Tarnower, or as cool as a mountain stream.

Before the gun was fired, the argument that occurred between these long-time lovers apparently degenerated into a physical contest, and the pain of blows to her face and arm could have led to her squeezing the trigger of the .32 caliber revolver and shooting Tarnower.

Then, conceivably, she could easily have continued to shoot at him without realizing she was doing so.

So much for the defense's position.

But why did Tarnower not see what was coming?

Why did he not make an effort to get the gun from her when he was hitting her? He knew her very well—he knew how she reacted to humiliation and pain. Why did he let himself be put in a position of complete defenselessness?

* * * *

Each of the two lovers made a crucial mistake in those most important moments that night in Tarnower's bedroom.

Hi Tarnower did not understand that Jean Harris was serious about ending her life—if, indeed, that was what she told him. If she came to kill him in cold blood, he did not believe she was serious about that, either.

His mistake was an inability to understand the deadly serious intent that was in Jean Harris's mind—whatever that intent.

His mistake was in, perhaps literally, turning his back on her.

Jean Harris's mistake was of another kind. Because of a number of signals she had been receiving from Hi Tarnower, Jean Harris may have thought that Hi Tarnower had ceased to love her.

That was her fatal mistake. She did not die from it; but she quite effectively ruined her life.

As his will proved, Tarnower *did* love her; had loved her for a long time. He loved her enough to leave her money. Money to Tarnower was material affection that he bestowed on those he loved and appreciated. The amount he bestowed on her belied the gossip of close acquaintances.

If Tarnower did leave Lynne Tryforos almost as much as he did Jean Harris, he still did not turn his back on Jean Harris. There was a large space in his heart devoted to her—a slightly larger space than was devoted to her rival.

Her mistake was in fearing she had lost his love.

* * * *

Aside from these two serious final mistakes, the lovers had made other mistakes even before the crucial confrontation.

Tarnower was wrong, for example, in not understanding fully the implications of his new relationship with Lynne Tryforos and of its effect on Jean Harris.

He had been described as a generally loyal man who did not play the field constantly.

In breaking his "game plan," apparently for the first time in his life, he had not only violated his own rules of conduct, but he had left undone things which he should have done.

Nothing is more difficult than breaking off an affair that has run its course—at least that is the opinion of experts who have played the field and survived.

But nothing is more essential to the success of an upcoming affair than a clean break with the last. When Tarnower failed to comply with that essentiality, he was leaving himself wide open to the kind of tug-of-war that two women can exert on a man.

Although Jean Harris tried to ignore the existence of Lynne Tryforos, as we must speculate from her actions, it was not an easy thing to do. And, eventually, the other woman's hold on Tarnower may have been one of the several upsetting factors that eventually goaded her into her final acts of desperation.

Maintaining liaisons with two women at the same time was a mistake Hi Tarnower should not have made. He knew better. It went against his code.

Yet apparently his love for Jean Harris was great enough to override his own common sense, his own instincts of survival, his own knowledge of psychology and of the woman he loved.

That was a secondary mistake—but it was a beaut.

Jean Harris made a secondary mistake, too.

We have to assume that in her torment she must have at some point come to the conclusion that she did not want to live any longer. The notes she wrote expressed the belief that she would soon be dead.

As a woman of direct action, conviction, self-assurance, if she wanted to kill herself, why didn't she take the gun she had purchased—for what reason no one can guess—and shoot herself with it?

Of course, it may well have been that she never considered killing herself. If she did, she might well have decided against it because it was contrary to her religious and personal convictions. Suicide may have had a definite aura of cowardice about it.

There are two other speculations it is possible to make in regard to the strange death of Hi Tarnower.

Suppose, for example, that Jean Harris throughout the entire ordeal—beginning March 9, say—was entirely clear-headed, purposeful, and cunning. Suppose she had originally purchased the revolver to kill Hi Tarnower because of his interest in Lynne Tryforos.

Suppose she deliberately pretended desperation in her notes and the long, rambling letter to Tarnower in a state of "confusion" which she purposely feigned in order to establish a distorted motive for her visit to Purchase.

Suppose she entered Tarnower's bedroom, pretended to be irrational, provoked a fight so she would show bruises, and then shot him to death.

We have only her word, and the word of others who heard her, that she had come up to Purchase to have Tarnower kill her. We have only the written material she may have designed to establish her confused state of mind.

This is a wild and far-out supposition. It doesn't explain away many details that keep cropping up. For instance, why did she struggle physically with Tarnower? She would be risking her own death. Why didn't she arrange a scene that might make a plea of self-defense possible? Why didn't she plan an adroit murder plot so she wouldn't even be implicated?

There are a pair of other wild suppositions that can be considered, too.

In Daphne du Maurier's *Rebecca,* the title character learns she is dying and goads her husband into killing her, thus saving herself from a painful suicide.

Could Jean Harris have planned to beg Hi Tarnower to kill her because she was fatally ill?

Or, to put the idea into the opposite perspective—could Hi Tarnower have found himself fatally ill and taunted Jean Harris with his womanizing to such an extent that she wanted to destroy him?

Impossible.

Tarnower was a man who was trying vainly to hang onto two women rather than one—the bequests in his will attest to that fact—and as a result failed to hang onto either one.

Whatever the real motivation, whatever the "intent" in the legal sense of whoever killed him—Hi Tarnower died of gunshot wounds and Jean Harris was accused of killing him.

It was, indeed, a strange death—a death that should never have happened at all.

15

The Rivals

There was a great deal of sympathy for Jean Harris from the public, once the story of the Tarnower triangle became public.

In addition to telegrams and letters, there was even a bit of money sent in. Jean Harris was not a highly-paid professional woman, even though she did hold down a prestigious job.

There was not enough money to pay for her defense. She did not even have enough money to pay for her hospitalization for psychiatric care, which was essential in view of her mental condition.

According to Joel Aurnou, her attorney, Jean Harris was refused admission to two hospitals because she did not have enough money to pay for her treatment, and was not covered adequately by medical insurance.

The third one accepted her at first, but later refused her, apparently, Aurnou said, because of the notoriety of her case.

She was eventually accepted at United Hospital in Port Chester, but the fact was kept secret until she had been discharged.

It was Joel Aurnou who set up what he called a "defense fund" on Saturday, March 15, five days after Jean Harris was arrested and arraigned to try to cover the difference between the medical bills and the insurance payments. He would also use the money from the fund for legal and investigative costs arising from the case.

No one wanted to guess how much the total anticipated costs for Jean Harris might be.

"There is no way she can afford it," Aurnou said. "She's a school teacher."

Some of the offers of money came to Aurnou from families of students or former students. Others came from personal friends. Aurnou appointed Jean Harris's son David, who lived in Yonkers nearby, to administer the defense fund.

Meanwhile, others had come to Jean Harris for exclusive rights to her story. The *New York Post* was said to have offered $25,000 for those rights. Aurnou said that the *Post's* offer was one of the "smaller ones," which included others he did not specify.

Exclusives on books with huge advance payments had also been offered, he said, but had not been discussed with his client.

"She has much more pressing psychological problems," he said. "The defense fund is a much more viable idea than book contracts. We don't intend to make money off this."

Telegrams and letters came in from all over the country.

Parents of a former student now living in Palm Beach, Florida, said, "We want you to know how much we care for you and love you. We have always supported your wise decisions at Madeira.

"We are sorry for not giving these assurances

to you personally, as we now realize how desperately lonely the role of headmistress must be.

"You have given our daughter a wonderful philosophy and outlook on life for which we will be forever grateful.

"No matter how lonely one must feel you have only to turn to the Bible to realize He cares for you."

A student from Alexandria, Virginia, wired her former headmistress:

"My warmest feelings with you in all these hard times to come. I will never forget the good you have given the Madeira Community. I have faith in the Lord and he will see you out of these trying times."

One telegram from Lexington, Kentucky, read:

"Please know that we are 100 percent behind you and send our love and full support. Let us know if we can help you in any way."

A telegram from Rockville, Maryland, read:

"Wishing you courage. Assuring you we are all with you in thought and in prayer."

Jean Harris was not able to read all those notes at the time they were sent to her, but she did read them as soon as she was able. Her state of mind during the first hours of her arrest was one described by some of those close to the family as "shock."

During the first days after the murder in Purchase, Jean Harris divided her time between jail and the home of a friend in Westchester County.

She would lapse in and out of "deep depressions," it was reported. When friends or family members talked to her she would appear to listen, but then all of a sudden, she would "go blank."

"She now cries at the drop of a hat," one close acquaintance said, "which is totally out of character."

It was for this reason that Joel Aurnou decided to have her admitted to the hospital for psychiatric care.

* * * *

And what about Lynne Tryforos, the "other woman"? There is no doubt but that she heard about Hi Tarnower's death in the very early morning hours of Tuesday, March 11. She appeared at his home on Tuesday, but was not questioned at the time by police.

Shortly after that, she discreetly vanished. She took her two daughters out of school, and went into seclusion for eight days. Police continued to report to the press that she would be questioned about the death of Tarnower, but did not specify exactly when.

She was indeed finally interrogated on Tuesday, one week and one day after Tarnower's death. The only glimpse the public got of her was in photographs taken by Jack Smith of the New York *Daily News* and an earlier picture of her with Tarnower in his office at the Scarsdale Medical Center that appeared in *People* Magazine.

Lynne Tryforos had always been a good friend of Tarnower's sister Pearl Schwartz. In fact, it was no secret among Tarnower's intimates that his sister preferred Lynne Tryforos to Jean Harris as a companion for her brother.

And, of course, Lynne Tryforos was at Hi Tarnower's house for dinner the night he died. With her, as guests, were Tarnower's sister Pearl and a niece.

Tarnower had a favorite among his three nieces. She was allocated more of the residue of Tarnower's will than the other two nieces and nephew. It is pure speculation, but it is a safe bet to assume that the fourth party at Tarnower's last dinner was his sister Pearl's daughter, Deborah Schwartz Raizes.

It is quite probable that these close relatives of Tarnower's were the ones who helped Lynne Tryforos maintain her privacy during the trying days just after his death.

She did appear unobtrusively at the funeral ceremonies, although neither the press nor the authorities actually saw her there.

Her questioning by police apparently went along very well and very surreptitiously. Assistant District Attorney Thomas Facelle, in whose offices she was questioned, said that she had been "extremely cooperative" during interrogation.

She was asked, presumably, about her relationship with Tarnower and the events leading up to his death. The interview lasted "a couple of hours," Facelle said.

He did not specify what the questions put to her entailed, and he declined to say any more about the session when pressed by members of the media.

Photographs of her show a very pretty woman, blonde, slim, blue-eyed, with an attractive, well-mannered appearance.

The tragedy of Dr. Herman Tarnower seemed to have affected her quite deeply, altering her obviously sunny expression and shadowing her face with lines of sorrow and sadness.

* * * *

In the ten days she was in the hospital, Jean Harris gradually regained her composure and looked to be in good health at her last court appearance in March—the felony hearing—when she was charged with second-degree murder.

It will be remembered that when Judge Couzens made the charge, he told her that she would be allowed to leave Westchester County for one trip to Virginia, where she could collect her belongings. Then she was to return to Westchester to await trial.

Jean Harris, with her son David, drove down to Madeira School. On the Saturday after her final appearance in court, ironically enough, as they drove through the rolling countryside of Virginia, they passed dozens of signs that are placed throughout the state:

"Virginia is for lovers."

For the first time since she could remember, the gate to Madeira School was locked.

David Harris's green Volvo station wagon was let through the gate, past the rolling fields where horses grazed, along an almost endless stetch of whitewashed fence that separates Madeira School from the woods around it.

Soon she and her son were in the headmistress's house—"The Hill"—and they were packing up boxes with books, letters, photographs.

She no longer had any right to be in the house, no longer was headmistress of Madeira School, no longer was a part of the posh girls' school she had tried to make a model of integrity and virtue.

Vacation would be over at the school on Monday—the three-week spring hiatus ended on Sunday—but some of the girls were coming back already from their homes at the same time Jean Harris was packing up for good.

One brunette senior in Levis and blue T-shirt asked the guard to let her through the gates.

"Why are the gates closed?" she asked.

"Because of what's happened . . . you know," the guard told her in a subdued voice.

"Oh, yes," said the girl. "It's too bad, but the school will go on."

The student attracted the attention of reporters who were covering the story of Jean Harris's last visit to Madeira.

"Are you concerned that all the publicity the school has gotten will injure its reputation or hurt your chances of being admitted to college?"

"No," the girl responded. "Madeira has always had a top reputation and I think it always will."

"Why did you come to the school?" the reporter asked.

"To ride," she said.

"No. I mean, why did you come to the Madeira School three years ago?"

253

The girl looked at the reporter. "To ride," she said again.

And Jean Harris and her son continued to pack boxes and put them in the car.

After noon David Harris was cornered by reporters at an off-campus McDonald's nearby, where he had gone to grab a quick takeout order for himself and his mother.

"How is your mother?" he was asked.

"Okay. But she could be better," David said. "She's very upset, very upset." He himself looked tense and upset.

"What is she doing back at the school?"

"She's packing," he said. "Packing to leave, packing up her life."

MOTHERS AND LOVERS
By Jeannie Sakol
Best selling author of "Hot 30" and "Flora Sweet"

PRICE: $2.25 LB743
CATEGORY: Novel

A witty, romantic novel of the intricate relationships between mother and daughter, husband
and wife, man and woman. Stephanie, twenty-
four, pregnant and on the verge of a divorce,
blames her mother Melissa for the mess she's in.
But Melissa's life has been no bed of roses either.
Stephanie finally realizes that no one is responsible for another's mistakes. She must solve her
own problems and fulfill her own destiny.

UNDER THE EYE OF NIGHT
By Robert E. Mills

PRICE: $2.25 LB718
CATEGORY: Occult Novel (Original)

If you can imagine the Godfather meeting the
Exorcist, UNDER THE EYE OF NIGHT is even
more terrifying! The mafia murders a young drug-
runner, whose father has black powers that he
turns against the mob. Then a series of bizarre
events threaten to destroy the once-powerful
family. One by one they are possessed by an
unspeakable evil, and one by one they die—a
dense fog envelopes one victim and kills him...the
sounds of a slurping beast follow another...a car
mysteriously fills with water and drowns another.
The force is more horrifying than anything the
mob could create—and totally beyond their
control!